Academy for Losers

By Cat Shaffer

Digital Release: December, 2015

Editor, Mark Shaffer

Cover Design by Fat Cat Books

This edition is published by Fat Cat Books, 920
Blackburn Avenue, Ashland KY 41101.

Chapter One

I knew it was going to be a bad day during first period biology class. Everyone else reanimated their frogs, no problem, while mine lay forever deceased in front of me. Mrs. Clarke tried to help; she always tried to help. But no matter what I said or did, that frog just stayed dead. So I wasn't surprised when I ended up sitting in a chair outside the principal's office as second period began.

I was shocked when I finally got called in and saw my mom and dad there. Mom's eyes were puffy, like she'd been crying. Dad had that look I hated, the one he gets when he feels sorry for someone.

Me, in this case.

Mr. Winters, principal at Green Hills like forever, sat behind his desk and sighed when I sat down between my parents. Mom took my hand, Dad patted me on the back and Mr. Winters said, "I hope you realize, Violet, how much your parents love you. Like me, they want what's best for you. After careful consideration, we've decided the answer may be a transfer to another school."

I recall him saying how everyone thought I was great, and no one in the school put out more effort than I did. What I remember most, though, is my mom starting to sob again when Mr. Winters began to talk about my future.

"It's really for the best," he said as if I wasn't even there. "She'll be with others of her kind and get the training she needs to be a contributing member to society."

Others of her kind? Like smart girls who aced every science class she took except, duh, the part of biology that brought frogs back to life. But if I was being sent to the charter school for future rocket scientists, why did my folks look so sad?

While I pondered, Mr. Winters opened a folder on his desk. A sheaf of pages floated over to Dad. Mom's grip on my hand grew tighter as Dad grabbed the papers and read them, sighing as he did so. Mom began to shake, and I realized she was big-time crying, like I was dying or something. So I stared at Mr. Winters to keep from looking at my folks and realized, not for the first time, how much he looks like a basset hound. In order to keep back the threatening giggles, I took deep breaths and stared at the plaque above his head given to him by the Convocation of Master Wizards in recognition of his 25 years as a school administrator.

I sort of lost the conversation between my parents and him as I subtracted 25 years from the current year. I'd always wondered if he was a thousand years old or just looked that way. I was so not ready when my mother let go of my hand, stood up and joined Dad at Mr. Winters' desk. She took the pen from him and wrote under where Dad had signed with his loopy cursive.

That was all it took. I never entered a classroom at Green Hills again.

"What do you mean, I'm changing schools?" I stared at my father, dismayed.

I turned to my mom, who was dabbing at her eyes with a tissue. "I can't leave. Mabry and I are presenting our version of the witches scene from 'Macbeth' in fourth period literature."

Mom stared sobbing again. Dad told her to take me to the car while he waited for the school secretary to bring the stuff from my locker. I wanted to clean it out myself, to tell everybody goodbye, but I knew by the look on Dad's face that was a no-go.

The trip from school to our house was almost scary. My father hung onto the steering wheel so hard I thought it might come off in his hands. Mom kept turning around in the front seat to smile at me. I kept thinking about that movie I saw on late night TV at Gillian's about all the women replaced with robots to make their husbands happy. Her fake happy face looked the same each and every time.

"Hurry and pack, honey." Mom practically shoved me up the stairs to my bedroom. "Dad wants to get on the road."

I didn't even have a chance to send a fast text or IM anybody as I prepared for my banishment. Dad leaned against the door frame, tapping his fingers on the wall.

"Only take what I really needed." Mom gave that same tight smile as I shoved the contents of my dresser into one suitcase and my favorite clothes from the closet into another.

"I'm proud of you," she said, sniffling a little. "We'll visit you, and time will just fly past. You'll make new friends. Before long, it will feel as if you've always gone to school there."

Dad's hands stilled and he announced we better go. Mom picked up one suitcase, and I took the other one, grabbing Alfredo on the way. I'd had Alfredo since I was a little kid. His bear fur was shabby, and the beret he'd worn when I first got him disappeared years ago. But Alfredo knew my secrets, and I needed him to provide a little piece of home.

"Do you really have to take that thing?" Dad scowled as I shoved Alfredo into my backpack.

"I'm sure every other child there has a sleepy bear, too," my mother said in a sharp voice. "Isn't it enough that she's going away? Do you have to make her feel like she's being punished?"

"Maryanne, not now!" Dad's voice was grouchy. Now I knew why they'd been arguing lately and stopped whenever I got near. Basset Hound Winters had been on their case. Yeah, my total lack of magical skills hurt the school's overall test scores. And no, I probably wasn't going to get any better. But the real reason he was getting rid of me was because Green Hills Specialty School was the best in the country in spells and levitation, hands down, and he liked the way people toadied up to him.

"Can't we just go?" I wanted to get out of town before school let out and my friends started calling me to find out (a) why I'd been called to the principal's office and (b) why I totally disappeared after that.

"Get in the car, Violet." Dad grabbed my suitcases and motioned with his head toward the door. Mom hugged me hard, like I was leaving for Mars or something. When she let me go, I felt the dampness of her tears on my shirt.

****

"This is hard on your mother, you know."

Dad finally spoke to me after driving forever toward the wilds of civilization. We'd spent the last twenty minutes on a road full of curves and overhanging trees that made me think about those movies where stupid tourists get lost in the middle of nowhere and end up dead. Not that it could happen to us. Just make-believe, right?

"Like it's so much fun for me."

Dad shot me one of those looks that are supposed to inspire fear.

"You know we only want what's best for you. Green Hills is a fine school, but not the only one in the country. I think you'll like the new one. Ah, here's our turn."

He pointed toward a small sign that read "Hampstead Manor" with an arrow pointing to the right. After we made that turn, the road got narrower and the trees got thicker, and I prepared myself for the inevitable stalling of the engine. Ten minutes later, we were pulling up in front of this big brick place with a black-and-gold sign right in front.

"Well, kiddo, this is it."

Dad read the sign out loud: "Hampstead Manor. An Academy for Success."

I knew what that sign really meant:
Hampstead Manor, Academy for Losers.

Chapter Two

"I'm sure you'll like it here, Violet."

Miss Willowood was the guidance counselor.
That's what the badge on her more than ample bosom
said. Now I knew what my grandmother meant when
being built like a battleship. That was a perfect
description of Miss Willowood: square no matter
which side you saw her from.

I pretended not to hear her puff as she led the
way up two flights of steps to the girls' wing. If the
main room didn't have 20-foot ceilings, the steps
wouldn't have had a turn in the middle, which Miss
Willowood needed to tackle the second flight. She
pretended we were stopping so I could admire the
view of the carved woodwork and marble floor, and I
liked her for that. It was so much better than hearing
a recitation about her arthritic knees and wheezing
lungs.

The upstairs hall was shiny wood with a long carpet runner in reds and purples. We kept going and going until Miss Willowood finally stopped and opened a door.

"You're lucky," she said. "This single just became vacant."

Why, I wondered. Had the previous occupant wanted to room with someone? Or had she languished, ridden by guilt in being such a failure, until she finally went completely nuts and wound up in a loony bin?

"The rules are right here," Miss Willowood said, handing me a gilt-edged book. "Don't hesitate to ask if you have questions. That's what we're here for after all."

I'd almost managed to get "thank you" out when she added, "Lunch is at eleven. Your vocational tests begin at noon, and don't worry. If your tests go past the dinner hour, I'll make sure a tray is brought to you."

"The dinner hour?" That was, what, six o'clock or something?

"Our evening meal is served promptly at half past six," she said. "You'll enjoy the food. Our cooks are terrific."

9

Leaning close, as to confide a major secret, she said, "They're natural cooks. You know. Non-magical."

Before I could begin to frame a reply, she was gone, trudging down the hall toward the stairs. I sat on the edge of the odd-sized bed and stared at the book she'd left behind.

The rules.

Those two words made me shiver. I thought the rules at my old school were bad; what would the discipline at a place for us "special" kids be like?

I flipped to the first page and began to read.

"The goal of Hempstead Academy is to give students time to discover their potential and the life skills to reach those goals. The lack of magical abilities is not a license for failure. The administration and staff is dedicated to fostering success in a homelike environment."

OMG, did Mr. Winters moonlight writing this stuff?

"Students are expected to maintain neat surroundings and good personal hygiene. Friendships, while important, should not be second to scholarship. Study time is paramount."

And then there was a whole bunch more. Being late to meals would bring demerits, failing to turn homework in on time would shave points off the final grade, a student possessing a banned item would lose all privileges. I slammed the book shut. The message was clear: If it's fun, don't even think about it.

"Hi." A head appeared around the door frame. "I wanted to wait until old Wishicould was gone."

"Wishicould?" I echoed.

"Yeah, as in wish I could get married." The whole girl was in my room now, taking in my small amount of luggage. "You should see how she acts every time a dad comes for conferences or parents' weekends. She gets sweet enough to make you puke.

"By the way, I'm Wendy. Like in Peter Pan. Pretty funny when you realize I've never levitated on my own even once in my life."

"Join the club. The closest I've come to flying is when I was six and rolled off the garage roof onto the trampoline."

Wendy giggled. "You did not!"

"Did. Got a lecture from my dad and a month of smother love from Mom."

11

"So where you from?" Wendy settled on the bottom of my bed. The puffy pink comforter bundled up around her.

"Three hours that way." I pointed south. "You?"

"Colorado. My father prefers to have his failure locked up far away from home."

Wow. Hard on herself much? I couldn't believe anyone's parents would send them a long plane ride away just to preserve the family reputation as happy and magical. Then again, I'd met her like three minutes ago. She might be loaded with screw-up potential.

"Why are you in here?" A second girl walked in without shooting a single curious glance my way. She made a beeline to Wendy and tugged her up from the bed. "You know the rule about newbies."

Wendy rolled her eyes and took off.

"See you after your tests!" she called over her shoulder as she disappeared from the room.

The rule about newbies. I eyed the gilt-edged book again. Like it or not, I'd better read the thing. I stuck my hand into my pocket to retrieve my cell phone and check the time. Oh, wait, I didn't have one anymore. Or a laptop. Modern communication was a sin here where our grades were probably sent to our folks by carrier pigeon. Or maybe that was too modern.

I picked up the stupid book and looked for the ban on talking to new kids. Yeah, there it was on page nineteen.

"Students are to refrain from socializing with new students until after the intake process is completed. Interaction must take place in the presence of staff."

I tossed the book on the dresser and flopped on my bed. This place thrived on boredom.

That was the décor of my room, and every other place I'd seen so far—early American boring. White walls surrounded me; dark brown tile covered the floor. The only color in this place was the bedspread, and I figured the reason it was pink was so the housekeepers knew it went in a girl's room. The boys—wherever they were—probably had matching blue ones.

Sighing, I went over and opening the brown drapes that I figured covered a window. It was. Too bad the view was the backside of the other wing and a whole bunch of pipes that probably took care of heating and cooling this mammoth place.

I shut the drapes and flopped down on the bed. I wanted to be home. I wanted to be on my own bed, staring at the posters on the wall that I'd picked out, listening to my favorite music through my red puffy headphones. I did not want to be stuck in this brick prison with a book of rules to memorize.

"Don't cry!"

I said the words out loud, like my own motivational lecture. That was one of my dad's favorite phrases, "Buck up." Thinking about him made me sob even more. I might have stayed on that bed all day and bawled if a noise like a sick cow hadn't filled the air.

"Lunch bell!"

The shout came from Wendy as she passed my door, shoved from behind by the girl who'd come and stolen her away. I took a deep breath and ran into the bathroom. A quick scrub of my face wiped away the tears along with my makeup. I was debating whether I had time to put some back on when I heard heavy footsteps and stepped back into my room. There was Miss Willowood, looking none too happy that she had to fetch me.

"I thought you'd follow the others," she said, snapping her fingers in a hurry-up gesture.

"Sorry," I mumbled. I fell into step behind her, wishing I didn't have to face the other students in one huge mass. I didn't know how many kids were here, which didn't help. This place was gigantic. I hoped there weren't tons of people sitting at long tables, all staring at me as I walked in.

"The dining room is down there and to your left," Miss Willowood said at the bottom of the stairs before abandoning me. Flashes of an old cartoon movie popped into my mind, and I saw Alice in her little blue dress hesitantly walking into Wonderland after she fell down the rabbit hole.

I knew how she felt.

"Over here!" One voice greeted me as I walked into the dining area, a waving hand demanding my attention.

Wendy was at a round table with four other people, two guys and two girls. Keeping my eyes on her, I walked over and sat in the only empty chair. That put Wendy on one side of me and the most incredible guy I'd ever seen on the other.

"Are you sure it's okay for me to be here?" I looked around for Miss Willowood coming to snatch me out of my seat.

15

"They have to let you eat. It's like the law. And this is the only open place." Wendy gestured across the table.

"That's Muffy and Molly, who'd be twins if they didn't have different mothers and fathers," Wendy introduced us. "The strong, silent type over there is Oliver. Or as we call him, Ollie."

Oliver tossed a wadded up napkin at Wendy, who ducked before it hit her.

"And that," she pointed across me at the gorgeous one, "is Razland."

She added something, but I couldn't hear what for a squeal that made me cringe. A disembodied voice immediately followed the noise, advising us that in honor of our new student, table three would go first.

"That's us." Wendy put a hand under my elbow and pushed me up. "We don't get to go first very often. One day we go in order, table one to ten, and the next day we go in reverse order, ten through one. Three is always stuck in the middle."

I did a quick calculation. Six people at a table, ten tables—sixty of us in all. Did that include teachers? I did a quick look-see as I walked to the serving line and realized there were two whole tables of them.

My parents would be delirious with this sort of teacher-student ratio. My mother was still convinced all I needed was a tutor and I'd be able to change her convertible from blue to purple if I wanted. I suspected that magic didn't run through our teachers' veins either. I mean, who would want to spend their time teaching us deficients a trade if they could have a good job in a real school?

A few people said hi as I walked past them. I said hi back, even though I felt weird doing it. I'd been going to school with my friends ever since we started pre-magic, and my besties were all at Green Hills. Starting school in six weeks in, stuck 24 hours a day with people who already had friends here, sucked. I felt tears prickle and swallowed hard. I was not going to cry. I was NOT going to cry.

"It gets better." Razland was beside me, taking my tray. Holding his in one hand and mine in another, he nodded at one person then another until we reached our seats. He set down our trays and then, much to my surprise, pulled my chair out for me.

My mother would be impressed.

"Wow, Raz, you managed to get all the way back here without tossing your spaghetti on anyone."

The teasing comment came from Oliver.

I glanced up at Razland, surprised to see his face turning red.

"He's gorgeous but a klutz." The ever-chatty Wendy was back at my side. "Part of it's those size twelve boats he calls feet, but mostly he's plain old clumsy."

"You don't have to tell everyone everything you know."

Raz's defense went south when he tripped on the leg of his chair and fell into his seat sideways. Oliver's bleat of laughter and the giggles coming from Muffy and Molly made his face turn even redder.

"Shut up and eat," he muttered, turning around and picking up his own fork.

When Wendy started giggling, too, I was sure I liked these guys. Their unrepentant faces when Miss Willowood barged up to scold us for interrupting the dignity of the dining room, even after she pronounced us a terrible influence for others, confirmed it.

And that's how I became part of the self-named Terribles, sworn to be friends forever.

****

Miss Willowood held me back when the bell rang and everyone left the dining room. We walked down the hall and turned right into another corridor, which, surprise surprise, had white walls and brown tiles on the floor. The room she showed me into was like to a parallel and much better universe.

This one had bright yellow walls, lots of plants and actual lamps instead of the long fluorescent lights that were everywhere else in this place. The most surprising thing in the room, though, was the tiny woman sitting cross-legged on top of the desk.

I was definitely impressed. She had to be older than my mother, and she was sitting like a kid. She made me like her even more when she made a shooing motion toward Miss Willowood so we could be alone.

"My last name is a mouthful, so I go by a short version." She unfolded her legs and slid off the desk. She really was tiny; her head barely got to my shoulder. "You can call me Miss Tiddums or you can call me the crazy lady, just don't call me late to dinner."

I giggled; she smiled.

19

"That's more like it," Miss Tiddums said. "I give extra credit for smiles, you know."

"Really?"

She sighed. "I wish I could. But I'd get caught, and my punishment would be to wash Miss Willowood's undies for a month."

Laughter rolled out of me. I tried to stop it by slapping both hands over my mouth, but the vision of Miss Tiddums scrubbing old lady panties on a ribbed washboard wouldn't leave my head. Miss Tiddums laughed with me, sounding like a kid herself.

"Unfortunately, we have to do something serious now," she said as our laughing tapered off. "Time for tests."

She tipped her head and studied me. I felt like a butterfly pinned on a display board as she narrowed her eyes, tapped her fingers against the desktop and sighed. Bending down, she brought up a plastic tote and plopped it right between the two of us.

"First test," she said. "What color is this?"

"Red."

"Excellent." She marked something in a long, slim notebook before reaching into the tote and pulling out Exhibit #2.

"And this is?"

"A ball."

Miss Tiddums lifted her eyebrows like she expected more.

"Blue. Rubber. The bouncy kind."

"Very good." Another note and another grab from the tote. "And this?"

I shrugged. "I don't know. It's in a paper bag."

"Guess," she suggested. "Fix your eyes on it and concentrate."

I tried. I narrowed my eyes until the world was a sliver of red tote and Miss Tiddums, reaching my hands toward it in the hopes that maybe I could do a distance feel and figure it out. But since distance feeling is a magic thing, I ended up with the same answer the second time she asked me what she held.

"I don't know!"

When her face softened, I knew she heard the frustration in my voice. *I* heard the frustration in my voice, even though I was trying to sound cool and unconcerned.

"If you did, then I'd have to recommend sending you somewhere else," Miss Tiddums said. "Without magic, there's no way you would."

Opening the bag, she stuck in her hand and came out with a foil-wrapped package. After peeling off the wrap, she took off layer two, the same kind of wax paper my mother uses to cool cookies on. The mystery object was an apple, which she deftly broke in two. She offered me half.

"You may want to nibble on this," she said. "Maybe it will take the memory of that lunch away."

I accepted my share and bit into its crisp, moist surface. Truly tasty, I decided as Miss Tiddums made short work of hers. I sped up my eating and finished quickly, too.

"Now time to work." Miss Tiddums disappeared below eye level of the desk, popping back up with a handful of colorful papers. I watched her sort them into individual piles, forcing back panic as I realized how many there were. Forget dinner; I'd be grateful to be done by the time the bell rang for breakfast.

"Let's start here." A stack of pink papers was plopped in front of me. A cup of newly sharpened pencils was soon beside it. "Take your time, but don't think. Check the first thing that comes into your mind and move on to the next question. In the meantime, I have a thriller to finish."

She pulled a paperback book with a crimson cover from a drawer and settled cross-legged on the desk again, oblivious as I turned the first page over and began to peruse it. I was happy to see wide margins and big print as I settled down to answer the multiple-choice questions.

By the time I'd gotten to the purple pages, the last ones left in the stack, Miss Tiddums was reading a different book and my fingers and mind were both numb. And my butt. A nice, soft recliner would have been mucho better than the wooden desk seat I'd been plastered to for four hours if the clock on the wall was right.

"All done," I sang out, glee filling me at the idea of being finished.

"Oh, good." Miss Tiddums marked her book with a slip of paper and slid off the desk. Shaking all over, like a dog after a bath, she pronounced the written portion done.

Stacking my completed forms, she said, "The orals will be snap after that."

Orals? OMG, there was more?

The questions came fast and furious without giving me time to think about anything. I parroted back some of the stuff I'd learned at Green Hills, the ins and outs of magical this and transcendental that. Finally Miss Tiddums shook her head and threw up her hands.

"My dear, this is not a test of what you've been taught but what you *know*. Deep down inside yourself, not having to think kind of knowing. Let's back up and try again."

This time I winged it, tossing out whatever my brain made my mouth say. I vaguely heard the bell for evening meal, but it was the same kind of background noise as the occasional hiss of the old radiator by the window. When we were finally done, the light outside was a vista of purple, red and orange, the most perfect sunset I'd seen outside the movies.

I was about to thank Miss Tiddums and go up to my room, hoping someone would bring me food for my growling stomach, when she held up a finger to keep me right there.

"Tonight's dinner is salmon patties and peas, I believe." She made the same kind of face as a baby did looking at pureed squash. "I detest both salmon patties and peas. Care to sneak away with me?"

Uh, oh. Stealing off campus on my first day at the academy even with a teacher—especially with a teacher—sounded sketchy, the perfect way to get in trouble. I was fumbling to find a way to say no without ticking her off when she clapped her hands and said, "Oh, dear, I didn't mean go get a burger. I have a lovely chicken roasting at my cottage with the most delicious seasonings. There's far too much for one person. Besides, if you join me I'll have an excuse to make mashed potatoes and break out the ice cream."

It was like she knew my absolute most favorite foods. Not that her mashed potatoes would be like my mother's, the best in the world, but even the worst mashed potatoes were better than the best peas. And fish…let's not even go there.

Without waiting for me to say yes or no, she grabbed a purple cloak and bright orange scarf, put them on and lifted the red tote bag. She picked up a phone I hadn't even seen when I came in, pressed some buttons and said, "I'm taking the new girl to Calliope Cottage. I think she'll feel more comfortable with the final interview there." She hung up before whoever was on the other end had a chance to say a single word.

For a woman her age, Miss Tiddums could move. Long steps let me keep up with her as we walked out of the building, down the sidewalk and onto a path of brick pavers. I managed to keep pace the short distance to her house. "Calliope Cottage" was a cute name, but it didn't look anything like a calliope. No big pipes, no metallic music pouring out when she opened the door…it was more like the gingerbread house of the witch in Hansel and Gretel. Bright pink curlicues sprouted from the wooden overhang and vines climbed a purple trellis at the end of the porch.

A wonderful aroma wafted out as the door opened, making my stomach grumble. Miss Tiddums must have heard it because she grinned over her shoulder at me and said, "Make yourself at home. Supper will be ready in a jiffy."

The inside of the house matched the outside. Bright afghans covered the deep, cozy chairs in her living room, and I could see a huge bowl of flowers on her dining room table. At Miss Tiddums' urging, I sat in one of the chairs, which, it turned out, happened to come with a cat.

"Flossy loves that chair," she said with a smile as the sleek black and white feline jumped on my lap. "And by extension, anyone who sits in it."

Since my folks were dog lovers, I wasn't used to cats. That was okay because Flossy seemed to be used to people. She circled on my lap a couple of times before curling up and starting to purr. I found myself relaxing as I stroked her soft, thick fur. Maybe I could guilt my parents into letting me have a kitten when I went home for the summer.

If I closed my eyes, I'd have been as asleep as the cat. The trip here, meeting the others, taking all those tests…this day had been as exhausting as any I could remember. Even my futile attempts to revive that stupid frog hadn't worn me out as much as everything I'd gone through in the last eight hours.

"White gravy or brown?" Miss Tiddums' voice called from the kitchen.

"Uh, white." I'm not sure the difference between the two, but it seemed impolite not to choose one or the other.

"Corn or green beans?"

Whoa, another question.

"Corn, I guess."

"Then corn it is," came Miss Tiddums' reply.

Flossy had begun to snore by the time Miss Tiddums finished fixing the meal. She gently picked up the cat and laid it on another chair without waking it. She must have had a lot of practice.

"Eat up!" Miss Tiddums speared a piece of golden-skinned chicken from the platter set in the center of the dining room table. I followed suit, adding some of everything else to my plate as well. I decided as soon as I took a bite that I'd died and gone to heaven, soooo much better than salmon patties. I tried to be polite and use my best manners, but when Miss Tiddums picked up her chicken to eat it, I did too.

Eating a meal with a teacher in her house should have seemed weird. But somehow it didn't. When she started asking me questions about what I wanted to do when I got out of school and what my hobbies were, I answered without thinking. We finished dessert, rocky road ice cream with fudge topping and whipped cream, before she smiled and said, "All done! I'll walk you back to your room."

Oh, wow, was she sneaky. If I'd known all those questions were part of the official testing, I might have thought before I spoke. I wondered now what she was going to tell whomever she reported to about the things I'd blurted out. Ah, well. The meal was worth whatever happened next.

Miss Tiddums led me on a different path back to the academy. I didn't like this one as well. It was kinda spooky, with high bushes on both sides and not much light leaking through. I'd have run if I'd been alone, but I figured nobody would mess with Miss Tiddums. She might be little, but I think she has a wide protective streak in her.

One thing for sure, I'd rather have her on my side than against me any old day.

Chapter Three

"Hey, you awake?"

Startled, I opened my eyes and saw Wendy by my bed, her white nightgown glowing in the moonlight coming through my window. Apparently she took my open eyes as a yes, plopping down beside me.

"Where were you so long?" she said in a half-whisper that let me know she wasn't supposed to be out of her room.

"At Miss Tiddums'."

Wendy's eyes widened. "On purpose?"

"Of course. I mean, why would I go there otherwise?"

"You know she's the school psychologist, right?"

Oh, I so did not know. The way I'd talked about everything, she probably already wrote "fruitcake" in my permanent file.

"What about your tests?" Wendy didn't wait for an answer.

I shrugged. "I dunno. I guess someone will tell me something tomorrow."

"You'll have to see Miss Willowood." Wendy made a face. "I remember the day she assigned me classes. It's blah, blah, blah about how you have so much potential and there's nothing wrong with you because there's nobility in every kind of work. Smile and nod every so often and you won't have to say anything. She loves to hear her own voice."

"What do you think they'll do with me?"

"Boring stuff. Old Wishicould likes girls to take cooking and secretarial classes. I guess she figures if we can't find a husband, we can always get an office job."

I had my life all planned out. Finish high school, go to college, get married when I'm twenty-five and have two kids, a boy and a girl, before I'm thirty. Until Wendy said that, the Academy for Losers was just a bump on my life path. Now it looked like being stuck here was like hitting a concrete wall.

"I better get back," Wendy said, sliding off the bed. "There's a bed check at midnight and again at four o'clock, in case you want to know."

Getting back to sleep after Wendy's visit was almost impossible. My mind kept running around in circles. Why had Miss Tiddums taken me to her place? What would Miss Willowood tell me tomorrow? If she thought my future was to be a line cook in some buffet restaurant, it would absolutely suck.

That made me think about my mom and dad, and how they'd set up a college fund. Tears prickled against my eyelids when I thought about my room at home and my locker at school that I decorated just the way I wanted it. I hated this place. I detested the idea of some adult shoving me into a box labeled Violet's Future. Most of all I wondered how I ended up being non-magical when my folks had oodles of it.

I snuggled under my blanket when I heard footsteps coming down the hall. I pretended I was asleep when the door opened and soft light came in from the hall. The door closed and the footsteps faded as whoever was doing bed checks went to finish their rounds. Covers over my head, I wrapped my arms around Alfredo and let the tears flow until I dropped into a dreamless sleep that lasted until a blast of sound woke me up.

It sounded like circus music on steroids, a tinny version of a vaguely familiar song. Suddenly the music stopped and a voice started talking to me. Jumping out of the bed, I looked around and saw a small speaker above the door I hadn't noticed moving in.

"Good morning, students." It was a guy voice, I was thought, although it was hard to tell. "It's time to rise and shine for another great day. Your cooks have outdone themselves; today you have a choice of grits or oatmeal along with eggs, sausage and biscuits. See you in the dining room in..." a slight pause and then "...thirty-three minutes."

Was he kidding? I had to take a shower, pick out the right clothes, do my hair and put on my makeup in thirty-three minutes? Grabbing my bath basket and a towel, I ran down the hall to the bathroom assigned to me and three other rooms. My speed paid off because I was almost done showering

33

by the time I heard others coming in. A fast flow of words let me know that Wendy was one of them.

I shouted hello toward the other showers when I stepped out of mine, wearing a towel and nothing else. My trip back to my room was fast, and I was out of my room and heading for breakfast with two minutes to spare. I wasn't surprised when everyone from our table was there except Wendy.

"She's always late." Razland joined the line behind me. "She used to get in trouble, but the faculty finally gave up on her."

I filed that little fact away. Not that she got away with tardiness, but that it was a regular habit of Wendy's. I figured I wouldn't be as easily forgiven, and the last thing I wanted to do was start my time here with black marks.

"Sorry, sorry." We were almost finished when Wendy slid into her chair.

"Hey, you're early," Oliver said. "I still have all my grits and half my milk to finish."

"Yeah, you probably need to go and start all over," Muffy said, grinning. "You might just get to first period on time."

As Wendy laughed it off, I decided I was at the best table ever, especially when I realized

Razland was watching me. He was so cute and nice, too.

Which made me wonder why he didn't have a girlfriend. Or maybe he did. He probably spent his evenings writing long sappy letters to her. Maybe they were already talking about getting married someday. I bet his girlfriend even had baby names all picked out.

"Hey, Violet, where'd you go?" Molly waved her hand in front of my face. My cheeks warmed up; I hated blushing but I did it all the time. Raz was smiling. He better not have any abilities because I'd have to find a different table if he knew what I'd been thinking.

"Oh, leave her be," Wendy said. "She gets her classes today."

A collective moan greeted her words. Now I was getting mucho nervous. Could meeting with the guidance counselor be that horrible?

The answer was yes, I discovered as I sat opposite Miss Willowood in her office with its white walls and brown carpet. The only personal item I spotted was one of those battery-operated desk fountains, water continually pouring over rocks, which made me super glad I'd gone to the restroom before I walked in here. Miss Willowood turned out to be a huge fan of charts. The results of my tests with Miss Tiddums were all translated to graphs and curves and blocks of black, white and gray.

I was so not surprised when my classes turned out to be basic food preparation, beginning sewing, home décor fundamentals, introduction to office machines and the ever-popular business math and English composition. I'd hoped for at least a botany class, which would let me escape to the great outdoors from the land of white walls, but that apparently was too much to yearn for. Miss Willowood handed me a piece of paper covered with her tiny handwriting and stood to conduct me to my first girly class ever.

"I realize this is a big change for you, dear," she said as she followed me out of her office and locked the door behind us. "It's very sad that your parents insisted you take advanced academic classes at your prior school. Here you'll learn skills to allow you to be self-supporting in case you never meet your Mr. Right."

Wendy's words flashed back to me about Miss Willowood's choices for girls. I bet she never even looked at my transcript from Green Hills. Or maybe she hoped I'd forget everything there, like chemistry and geography. She probably figured that since my magic wasn't up to par, my brain wasn't either and I'd be lucky to find my way around my own house without a map. I plastered a smile on my face and trotted along, pretending I really cared about the wonderful opportunities for cake decorators these days.

The student kitchens were in a corner of the basement, down the hall from the woodworking area and across from a door marked "Janitorial Staff Only!" Being forbidden to enter made me so want to take one little look inside, but I knew better with Wishicould only inches from me. The aroma of cinnamon and vanilla wafted out when she opened the door to the classroom, where all heads turned to stare at the newcomer.

"Come in, come in." The teacher looked nothing like I expected a cooking teacher to look. She was tall and skinny and wore pearls and open-toed high-heeled shoes. She had a sleek French braid, but the look on her face was friendly. "We're about to make éclairs."

My mood went from bad day gloomy to bright and happy at those words. I love éclairs almost as much as I love blueberry doughnuts and apple fritters. If we made them, we'd get to eat them, right?

I noticed a hand waving frantically from the right side of the room as Miss Willowood turned me and my class assignments over to the teacher. The hand belonged to Muffy, who called my name as soon as the door closed behind Miss Willowood. At the teacher's nod I hurried over and took the kitchen stool next to her.

"You're going to love this class," she whispered fast, as the teacher started talking again. We were measuring out flour and counting eggs before I had a chance to ask about our teacher.

"She's cool," Muffy said, her voice low. "Lets us call her Dorothy and never yells when we mess up."

Which was a very good thing, since my mother ruled our kitchen and I only got to lick the beaters after she made a cake or help with pancakes on Father's Day. But I figured hey, I got a respectable B in first-year chemistry and following a recipe is like using a formula, right?

Wrong. So, so wrong.

"Hold it over the bowl!" Muffy squealed as I began turning the little crank on the metal sifter she'd handed to me.

"What?" I turned toward her, not sure what she wanted me to hold where.

Instead of answering, Muffy grabbed the bowl off the counter and stuck it beneath the sifter. It was too late. Misty white flour billowed through the air amid a collective gasp from the other kids. Every part of my body froze except my stupid hand, which kept turning the little crank while fine powder sprayed from the mesh bottom. By the time I managed to stop, Muffy had begun to giggle. I tried hard to ignore her, but when she wheezed out "You look like a ghost!" I was a goner, too.

Dorothy was trying hard to keep her teacher's face in place as she rushed over, but I could tell she was ready to laugh too. I dropped to the floor and started sweeping the flour up with my hands.

"Leave it, we'll get the broom." Dorothy tugged me to my feet. "Why don't you preheat the oven and get the baking sheets ready while Muffy and I work with the ingredients?"

Grateful for the politest reprimand I'd ever gotten, I read the instructions again. I couldn't fail another time. Absolutely couldn't.

Muffy hovered over me like a mother hen with a not-too-bright chick until our éclairs were on a plate and waiting for approval. Even though my contribution was teeny tiny, I still felt a swell of pride when Dorothy pronounced them perfect and told us to sample our dish. For the first time in a long time, I'd done something right.

I should have known *that* wouldn't last.

****

The office machines instructor wore black pants, a white shirt, suspenders and a bow tie. He sat behind his desk until we were all in the room and properly seated behind our desks. Trying to be discreet, I sneaked a look at the equipment along the walls. I had expected a computer and some calculators but these were big hulks of plastic and digital readouts. Right then I realized that the definition of "office machines" was more than a flash drive and scanner.

"Good morning, students," Mr. Alpert said. His name was written at the top of the white board behind his desk.

"Good morning," came a chorus of replies.

He looked right at me and said, "You'll notice we have a new student among us today. Please afford her the courtesy of not acting as if she's from outer space. I'm sure she'll answer your questions after class. Now, however, I would like your attention."

Way to go, Mr. Alpert. Could you make me even more freakish by making sure everyone saw me slumped in my seat trying to be invisible?

He passed papers to everyone but me, so I figured they were graded tests or homework. That made me a little paranoid right there. Since I didn't know a friggin' thing about this stuff, and they already had weeks of study, I might not be able to catch up. Then again, button pushing was probably the lifeblood of working with these machines, and I could do that. Maybe.

"Miss Greene."

It took me a second to realize Mr. Alpert was talking to me. I stood.

"Please help me demonstrate the refilling of toner and paper on this reproduction machine."

That was a fancy name for a copier I realized when he led me to this monster with like six trays and a control panel like a jet plane. Putting what I hoped was a convincing smile on my face, I watched Mr. Alpert open this, push that and slam the other. My heart started pounding like a racehorse when he suggested that I try it.

He didn't look like evil incarnate. With his blond going to white hair, rolled-up sleeves and that bow tie, he looked friendly. Like the guys who dish out ice cream at that restaurant at the mall. He nodded toward the machine, and after a deep breath, I set out to duplicate his movements.

Failure is too mild a word for what happened next. I thought I opened the right door and pulled down the correct plastic tab, but all of a sudden, the machine began to hiccup, and black powder sprayed over me, Mr. Alpert and the floor. Shaking the toner from his sooty sleeves, he shouted, "The kill button!"

Like I know a kill button from a doughnut hole. The only thing I could see was a red button so I slammed it with my hand. Instead of stopping, the stupid copier began announcing my sins.

"Toner cartridge is expended," the monotone voice repeated until an orange button lit up. The announcement became "Drum overheat warning, drum overheat warning, drum overheat warning" and the other kids in the class had their hands over their ears. I started punching all the buttons, which resulted in paper flying out of the top tray in a blizzard of legal-size sheets. Mr. Alpert dropped to the floor and crawled behind the stupid thing. Suddenly an awesome silence filled the room and he stood up, unplugged power cord in hand.

"Thank you, Miss Greene," he said in a voice that sounded anything but thankful that I'd joined his class. "You may take your seat."

I heard some giggles as I walked, head down, to my desk. I'm not sure whether they were laughing at me or Mr. Alpert, but I wasn't going to make eye contact. I'd had enough humiliation for one day.

I stiffened at the tap on my shoulder from behind me. I stared straight ahead as a boy's voice whispered, "Go out the back door. Old Alpert looks pretty ticked."

Having come in the door by the white board and not bothering to look around, I didn't know there was a second means of escape. But I'm smart enough to know good advice. The bell was still ringing when I slid into the group and took off for freedom, which, in this case, was the hall full of kids.

When I felt a bump and then a foot step on mine, I wasn't surprised to look up into Razland's

43

face. I waved him off when he started to apologize. We didn't have time for this.

"I screwed up."

He followed as I moved over to the side of the hallway and the words poured out of me. "The teacher asked me to do something and I didn't know how and now he's a mess. I mean it's my first day and he has to think I'm like truly stupid."

"Alpert?" Razland held up a hand to stop me.

"Exactly." I turned so my back was to the crowd and I was looking up into Razland's face. His smile was what I needed after the last two periods.

"It gets better," he said.

"Good because it can't get much worse. At least at my old school I could fake sometimes. Here everybody can see what a failure I am."

I told him about the flour and the toner and how these clothes might never get clean again. Then the bell for the next class rang, and he left me with a quick "Hang in there" and took off toward a door at the end of the hall.

My class, it turned out, was right across from where I was. I walked into a room with long tables, a dozen sewing machines and eleven girls. I took the only place left and smiled brightly at everyone. Maybe this would turn out to be my forte.

Or not. Knowing what a needle and thread are used for didn't help much as the plump instructor wandered through the room as she lectured. Her thoughts were as scattered as her movements. She went from telling us the history of textiles to her mother's creative use of cloth placemats to how much it hurts to run a sewing machine needle through your finger. I kept my hands in my lap and my feet pulled back. I was not, repeat not, going to embarrass myself again.

I was even a little excited when she said we were going to make purses. When she told us to sketch designs, mine came out like a boutique creation. Although my drawing skills aren't up there with Rembrandt, I managed to create a silk bag with a chain handle and decorated with fringe, spangles and lace skull and crossbones. It was, I decided when we all had to show our plans, the coolest ever.

Turns out that I'm the only one who thought so. The other girls began trashing my design, talking about lack of focal point and inadequate dimensions. I wanted to jump in and tell them theirs looked like cereal boxes covered in cloth, but I managed to keep my mouth shut for once. I was especially glad I had when the teacher okayed theirs and asked me to stay after class to talk about mine.

This was the first time ever that I had to stay after class. At Green Hills I managed to get by even without magic. My first day here and I was already in trouble with the one teacher I hadn't gotten messy.

"Sit, please sit." The teacher, whose name I still didn't know, motioned to the end of one of the tables. She sat cross from me and revealed her identity. Mrs. Tottenschott, she said, Tilly Tottenschott. I fought hard not to laugh.

Mrs. Tottenschott laid my sketch on the table between us, smoothing it with her hand.

"I love this," she said. Her eyes looked soft, like she was remembering something. "Creativity is supposedly prized here, yet we're expected to stifle it when it comes along."

She shook her head, and her eyes looked like, well, teacher eyes again.

"The other girls have had the assignment for a week, which is to create a functional handbag that can be mass produced," she said. "The academy's goal is to turn out well-rounded students with skills

46

that benefit them in their adult life. Fashion and accessory design fall within that area."

She traced a finger along the skull and crossbones one more time before folding my sketch and tucking it into her pocket.

"Let me give you some graph paper," she said. "If you have time tonight, play around and see if you can come up with something that meets the specifications. Neat and simple."

Boring, I thought but didn't say out loud. Mrs. Tottenschott actually seemed to like me.

****

By study time I felt like I'd survived a triathlon. My head ached from trying so hard not to screw up, and I had enough homework assignments to keep me busy until midnight or after.

Dorothy had provided me with a list of cooking terms to memorize before the next class, and Mr. Alpert had found me after sewing and handed over several machine manuals. I'm sure he plans to repeat today's exercise tomorrow and he doesn't want to look like a chimney sweep this time.

Business math was a whole bunch of story problems, which I've always hated, and the English class meant I had to read six short stories just to catch

47

up with the other kids, and then use their fundamentals to write my own short story. As soon as the last period bell rang, I escaped and headed to my room. I leaned against the closed door, determined not to cry but missing my family, my own room and my old school so much it hurt.

Why did I have to be born this way? Magic was finger-snapping simple for everybody I knew except me. I hated being different and I double hated being here.

Now I knew why cell phones were banned. I closed my eyes and imagined punching the numbers that would ring into my parents' house. I could almost hear the pleasure in my mom's voice when I said, "Hi, it's me" and her shout to Dad to pick up the other phone.

Dinner here could be steak and chocolate-dipped strawberries, but it couldn't taste as good as Mom's tuna casserole eaten at the table with her and Dad. This time when one of them asked how school was, I'd tell them everything instead of muttering, "It's okay." And if Dad wanted to know if his two best girls wanted to go out for ice cream for dessert, I'd be the first one in the car.

I remembered what Wendy said about how everybody felt lost here at first. Knowing that did not make me feel one bit better. I figured out in my head how long it would be until summer break and almost cried Thinking of two whole months with my parents made me even more homesick and even more certain that nothing good could come from my being banished to this place.

Much as I adored wallowing in my own sadness, I knew leaning against the door all night wasn't going to change a thing. I flopped on the bed with that list of cooking terms and tried to immerse myself in new knowledge. It didn't help. When the dinner bell rang, it was like a reprieve from the governor. Sitting around with Wendy and the others would be good.

Naturally, my disaster in cooking class was the featured entertainment. Muffy added a dramatic note that had everyone else laughing more than the moment was worth. But I knew they really were laughing with me, not at me, like that old saying goes. I actually felt okay by the time we finished our mystery meat and broccoli slaw and went back for our chocolate cake. Friends will do that for you.

My good mood lasted until lights out.
Tomorrow morning it all started over again. I had to
go back to the same stupid classes with the same kids
I didn't know watching for my next mistake.

Chapter Four

The day started so much better than I thought.
Breakfast was the usual—crappy eggs and grey swill
in a bowl with toast on the side—but Ollie's news
made me all bubbly inside.

"Ten more days until parents' weekend," he
announced.

Parents' weekend? My parents got to see me
here in prison, uh, boarding school?

"Sorry, Wendy," Raz said as he slid into the
seat next to me. "You can share mine if you want.
You know my mom. Smother love personified."

That's when I remembered that Wendy's
family was out west and she was stuck here in Ohio.
So maybe that always-happy mood was covering up
the same stuff I'd been hiding. I knew my mom and
dad would come once they knew. Mom would bring
my favorite cupcakes and Dad would call me one of

51

the silly nicknames he had for me when I was a little kid. I blinked back tears. I missed them so much.

"So how are your classes?" Ollie asked as he grabbed a slice of toast from Muffy's plate.

I shrugged. "Classes."

I was not going to tell anyone that I was approaching legendary failuredom in my first week here. Girls were supposed to know how to cook just like guys were supposed to know how to nail things together. That's the way the world was, with or without magical abilities.

Just thinking about cooking class took away the good feeling I'd gotten from learning about parents' weekend. Whatever she expected us to do, I was so not going to sift anything that formed into clouds.

Dorothy actually smiled at me when I walked into the room, and the other kids didn't giggle or point at me, so I figured the sifter incident was history. When Dorothy said we were going to cook and not bake, relief rolled through me. Anybody can use a fry pan, right?

Turns out the answer is no. It all looked so easy when Dorothy demonstrated making omelets.

Eggs in the skillet, stuff inside of them and flip. Any dummy can do that.

Some of the omelets were restaurant menu perfect. Muffy's was a little lopsided, but I could imagine it on a plate with some home fries and bacon. And then there was mine.

My experience in cooking breakfast is taking something from the freezer, sticking it in the microwave and sliding it onto a plate when the timer goes ding. Or, if I was in a hurry, throwing a toaster pastry into the toaster and eating it on the run. None of these required a stove, a spatula or hot oil.

The kitchen had a half-dozen stoves so six of us could cook at a time. I was in the second crew, which meant Muffy was sampling hers, and everyone else's, while I was making mine. Dorothy watched me get the eggs ready and pour them into the pan before she went down the line checking on everyone else. I tried to remember exactly how Muffy had made hers. She'd lifted the omelet and checked the bottom for sure, so I did that.

Afterward, it occurred to me that I probably should have held the handle of the pan. But I didn't. I stuck the metal spatula under the eggs, lifted them a little and yelled when the pan went skittering off the stove and across the tile floor toward Dorothy's feet. I yelled even louder when the spatula hit the red-hot burner element and the oil on it started to smoke.

I've never seen anyone move as fast as my teacher did. She shouted at me to drop the spatula and move away, grabbing that pan handle at the same time. My half-cooked mess slid out of the pan and across the floor, a gooey trail of eggs, green peppers and yellow cheese. When I started to cry, everyone rushed toward me offering sympathy and napkins.

What I wanted was to disappear. Melt through the floor or, if I was normal, blink or something and evaporate into thin air. But there I stood, totally humiliated, a big stupid dork who can't even flip eggs.

"It will be all right, Violet." Dorothy put her arm around my shoulders and led me away from the scene of the crime. I saw Muffy from the corner of my eye as she dropped down with paper towels and spray cleaner. I owed her another one.

I listened as my teacher delivered the obligatory "don't give up" speech even though I knew it was never going to get better. Two days, two disasters. I was gaining speed on my downhill slide.

****

Clutching the machine manuals to my chest, I sneaked into Mr. Alpert's class at the last minute and slid into my seat hoping he wouldn't notice me. Yeah, like that worked. He looked up from the attendance book, snapped his suspenders and said, "Nice to see you again, Violet."

"Glad to be here," I mumbled. Right now would be a great time to discover my secret ability to sink through floors.

"I hope you're prepared to show us how to use the XS6000." He stood and gestured toward the mammoth machine at the back of the room. Like puppets on a string, we all turned our heads at the same time to stare at it. I'm pretty sure I was the only one whose stomach dropped at the sight of it. Yeah, I'd looked through those books last night but I hadn't studied them. I'm not good with that figure A and pie chart B thing; the manual for the XS6000 had been nothing but diagrams and numbered instructions.

I turned back toward the front and gave Mr. Alpert my biggest, brightest smile. I was figured he was goofing with me. He didn't really expect me to tame that monster overnight. Or did he?

The answer was "yes" as it turned out. All eyes were on me as I trudged down what seemed an endless aisle to the XS6000 and stood beside it, ready to face my doom.

"Please demonstrate its abilities to sort, collate and staple."

I swallowed hard against the lump in my throat and fought down the urge to scream and run from the room. The power thingie glowed a malignant green. I swear it pulsed with evil intent as I took a first tentative step toward its control panel's five million buttons.

What had Mr. Alpert said? Copy, sort and collage maybe. Except I didn't have anything to copy. And how could I make a collage on this thing? I remembered the staple part, but what was I supposed to staple?

I blinked hard. I absolutely was not going to cry. I was a person, and that was a machine, and I knew I was smarter than any machine.

"Check the memory file."

I jumped at Mr. Alpert's voice behind my left shoulder. Memory file…memory file…with all those buttons there had to be one for that somewhere.

"Front left corner."

Left, left, left, I chanted to myself as I moved my shaking hand toward that button. I felt Mr.

Alpert's stare like a laser boring a hole in my back. I cringed as my finger made contact and the XS6000 came to life. A low rumble, a high-pitched beep and it started to do something. A red light flashed as the stupid thing asked from its digital display "Proceed with job?"

No. Do not proceed with job because I have no idea what I'm doing. For all I know the preloaded job has been booby-trapped by Mr. Alpert for revenge. The room was completely silent; the atmosphere was one of anticipation. Taking a deep breath for courage, I pressed the button in the right rear corner, the one emitting a steady green glow. At Mr. Alpert's sharp intake of breath, I knew it was the absolute wrong button. But once again, it was too late.

"Cancel!" he commanded, like I had a single clue how to do that. While I was trying to figure out if it was the triangle button, the stop sign-shaped one or the square one smack dab in the middle, it kept on running. Zip, zip, zip goes the XS6000 while pages of paper streamed out and Mr. Alpert freaked behind me. His arm snaked around me and hit the triangle button.

I stepped back as he started grabbing the pages from every output tray, muttering to himself. I tried to sneak a look at what I'd accidentally printed out and only caught glimpses of phrases like "he pulled out his Glock" and "I eat guys like you for breakfast." Although I may not be fast to catch on, I still realized Mr. Alpert was writing a book. On school equipment, it looked like, which I think was something he was not supposed to do.

I didn't bother with an apology. Running back to my desk, I grabbed my stuff and kept on going all the way to Miss Willowood's office. This was definitely one time when I wanted to get there first.

"I need to change classes." I dropped into the plastic student chair across the desk from her.

Miss Willowood raised an eyebrow. "Which one?"

"The ones that make me do something besides sit at my desk."

Miss Willowood leaned toward me. "The goal of this academy is to provide you with a top-notch education, which includes vocational training. You simply must understand that your path in life is different than your former peers. The sooner you accept who you are, the better your life will become."

If I had been magical, her head would have been on fire before she got the last word out. I was not a dummy. My IQ tests showed I'm smart, probably lots smarter than her. But she had a certificate on the wall so she was so special. Or thought she was anyway.

I forced my mouth to keep smiling even though I was fuming inside. Parents' weekend was only a few days away. Dad would fix things for me. Dad always fixed things for me.

Miss Willowood kept talking, but I quit listening. I nodded every now and then and said "Uh huh," and figured we were done when she leaned back in her chair. I made my escape without saying goodbye. Since lightning didn't strike me, I must have done okay.

The anger I was holding back erupted as soon as her door slammed behind me. Everyone else was still in class, so nobody heard me as I stomped down the hall toward the girls' restroom. I don't know how I looked, but I felt like one of those cartoon characters with steam coming out of my ears, I was so mad. And because I was mad, and the hall was deserted, I wasn't ready for what happened next.

Wham! All of a sudden I was on my butt, staring at a red-faced Razland who was sprawled beside me.

"I'm so sorry." He scrambled to his feet and offered me a hand to pull me up. My books were scattered across the floor mixed up with the papers he'd been carrying. He apologized the whole time we cleaned up the mess until I couldn't take it anymore.

"It wasn't your fault." I put my hands on his arms and stared into his eyes. "Really."

When he started to apologize again, I cut him off. The whole story spilled out, my mess with the omelet and my total spaz moment in Mr. Alpert's class and then Miss Willowood's lecture.. Raz tried hard to keep a straight face, but he couldn't. And by the time I finished, I was laughing too. Then the bell rang.

"I've got to get these reports to the office," he said, "but we're going to talk about this later. Okay?"

I nodded and headed toward math class. At least I couldn't screw up there; that kind of pi I knew all about.

****

Raz was waiting for me outside the dining hall. He looked a little worried until I smiled at him and he smiled back. He was so cute.

"The rest of the day go better?" he asked as we walked in for dinner.

I nodded. "Yeah. Except I have to write a five-page paper on the most influential person in history before Friday."

"Tough."

We didn't talk anymore about my horrendous morning because the others were at the table when we got there. Of course Muffy had to recap the cooking class disaster for everyone else, but it didn't seem quite so bad when she told the story. Luckily, none of them had witnessed my second black moment of the day, and I didn't mention it either.

"You're going to have to order carryout your entire life," Wendy said when Muffy finished the tale. "Or hire a spectacular cook."

"Maybe Old Wishicould can be my housekeeper," I blurted out, the memory of her dressing down still vivid.

"Ooh, she'd make you worm casserole and put sand in your sheets," Ollie said, bringing laughter from everyone again. As if the mention of her name had summoned her, Miss Willowood bore down on our table with a frown on her face.

"Aren't we a little noisy tonight?" she asked.

I had the perfect retort on the tip of my tongue like "Don't know about you, but we're just having fun." I was wise enough not to say it though. I could tell by the looks on the faces of my friends they were thinking the same thing. But we all apologized and she left.

For once dinner was not too bad. So we didn't talk much as we ate our barbecue sandwiches, slaw and potato salad. As we gathered our dirty dishes, Raz whispered, "Meet me by the library after lights out" to me and took off before I could say yes or no.

Time dragged as I did my homework and wondered how much trouble I could get into. I was the new kid, after all, and Miss Willowood had already made it plain I wasn't on her list of most-loved students. Struck by a sudden inspiration, I left my room and headed for Miss Tiddums' office.

Luck was with me. She was packing things into a bright orange tote bag, humming to herself, when I tapped on the door and walked in without waiting for an invitation.

"Violet!" Pleasure colored her voice. "I am so pleased to see you."

You'd think that the last person I'd want to confide in would be the school head shrinker. Miss Tiddums was different. The stress of the last couple of days started to fade as I sat in the bright room. When she asked one simple question—"How are things going so far?"—my frustration poured out of me. In a good way, though.

When I was done, Miss Tiddums rubbed between her eyes with two fingers like she was thinking hard. I just sat there, feeling the best I had since I'd gotten here. It was kinda like those talks I'd have with Mom when everything in my life sucked.

I was feeling so much better that I almost forgot what I'd come for.

"I have this really important paper and the library closed before I could get all my research done," I said, keeping my eyes wide open so she wouldn't know I was fibbing. "Even fifteen minutes on one of the computers would keep me from flunking for sure."

Miss Tiddums smiled and shook her head.

"You really shouldn't lie, dear. Your face gives it away."

I bit my lower lip as the bad feelings returned. Miss Tiddums had been nothing but nice to me, and in return I was trying to use her to keep my butt out of trouble.

"I'm assuming you have a good reason to try." She took off her coat and set the tote bag on the desk. "I also assume you'd rather do this research after room check."

"I'm sorry," I said. "Don't worry about it."

Miss Tiddums reached over and patted my shoulder. "It so happens that I have spent the whole day trying to remember the lines of a poem by Robert Frost. I don't think it would be a problem if you used a computer in the technology section while I wandered the non-fiction shelves."

When she winked, I was sure she knew I wasn't going to be there alone. But she didn't ask any more questions, and I didn't volunteer any more information. In a way, I felt better knowing she'd be around. Not like I didn't trust Raz, which I did, but just because.

****

Miss Tiddums slid a shiny gold key into the hole, and the lock opened. I followed her and waited as she flipped on a minimum of lights.

"I'll be right there." She pointed toward the opposite corner of the room from the banks of computers. "I'd say it will take, oh, twenty minutes to find what I need." She began to walk away and then turned back to me with a wide smile. "In case someone else comes to do research, remember I'm not that far away. Just the right distance for a chaperone."

In order to make my excuse not a total lie, I sat down at a monitor and logged on. I'd barely typed in "influential people in history" when Raz slid into the seat beside me.

"Hi." His voice was low, not quite a whisper but almost.

"Hi yourself," I whispered back.

"Are you okay?" He still sounded worried like he had in the hallway.

"Better now."

"What are you going to do?" He leaned toward me, his elbows on his knees, and my heart gave a little flutter. I shrugged.

"You don't have to stay in those classes, you know."

"Go tell Old Wishicould that."

Raz rolled his eyes. "Oh, come on. You scared of her? She's like one of those yappy little dogs celebrities carry around, all bark and no bite. Think of her tucked into a furry pink purse and you'll feel a lot better."

I giggled. I couldn't help it. The image of Miss Willowood rolled up and stuck inside a designer bag, her legs hanging out one end and her head the other, was too much to resist. Raz laughed too, a rumbling sound that made me happy.

"Seriously, you can take something else. The curriculum requires two-thirds of your classes be vocational training, but it doesn't have to be something you hate."

"Not hate, just suck at," I said. "Although I do kinda hate the XS6000."

He pressed on, asking me what I liked to do and what I didn't. I had to think in a different way. My parents had expected me to go to college, so all the clubs I'd belonged to were academic ones. My considerable skills in quick recall and chess were so not going to help me now.

"I'm totally useless." I folded my arms on the computer desk and laid my head on them. "I guess I should be glad I'm not dealing with living things because they'd never survive if I had to be in charge."

"Come on, you have to have mad skills at something." Raz leaned down and looked right at me. "Are you good with money? You could take accounting maybe."

"I told you I'm not good at anything." I closed my eyes so I didn't have to see the trust in his.

"So if you're not good at anything, come be bad with me."

I open my eyes and raise my head. "Like?"

"Like you should take small engines with me."

I stared at him. He was completely insane. The closest I'd ever come to a lawnmower was going along with my dad when he bought gas for ours. Besides, Miss Willowood had already made it plain I was stuck where I was.

"Are you ready, dear?" Miss Tiddums' voice came from a little way over. Raz jumped up, whispering, "Think about it" as he scooted around the computer bank and toward the door. Miss Tiddums' footsteps came closer.

"Almost," I called back, bringing the screen back to life. I was printing off stuff about George

67

Washington when she came to stand beside me. I could tell by the little smile on her face she knew I hadn't really been doing research and I hadn't been alone. She pulled out the chair next to mine and sat down.

"Would you like to tell me what's really going on?"

Busted. Since I was such a lousy liar, I decided I might as well confess. She listened as I told her Raz and I had been talking, and he thought I ought to switch into different classes, too.

"Let me think about this a little." She patted my forearm. "I promise things will get better. Now we'd better get you back to your room."

Even though no spies lurked in the halls, I still felt better having her beside me. Once I was ready for bed, I settled down with Alfredo curled in my arms and everything Raz had said on my mind. I couldn't do much worse with his engines than with the ones old Willowood had given me. Could I?

****

Friday morning was gloomy and rainy but I didn't care. My parents were coming to see me! I knew for sure because Miss Willowood had stopped me in the hall to tell me about the process. About all I remember of her blah, blah, blah was that the welcome reception started at seven p.m. and I could spend Saturday afternoon off campus with them. Ollie told me that after a while I could be with them the whole day, maybe even the weekend.

I used to wish I could go to boarding school waaaay away from home where my parents wouldn't have a clue what I was doing. Now that I was here, all I wanted to do was be at home, in my own bedroom, eating my mom's chicken tacos. Funny how life worked that way. Sometimes the thing you wanted wasn't nearly as great as you figured once you got it.

"How many ways can you serve oatmeal?" Muffy sighed as we sat down with our trays.

"With blueberries, strawberries, brown sugar and maple syrup," Wendy suggested.

"With raisins and walnuts," Molly added.

"Cutup bananas," I contributed.

"Enough!" Ollie threw up his hands. "I think the question was rhetorical."

"Here's a real one." Raz plopped his tray down. "Should Violet stay in the classes old Wishicould assigned her or change out?"

"Change. Definitely." Ollie nodded, his spoon of cereal tipping up and down with his head. "All that sappy niceness is a disguise. Inside she's mean and she gave you stuff she knew you'd do bad at."

I frowned. Could that be true? I remembered Miss Tiddums telling me to be patient and realized her remark about things getting better wasn't some empty thing school psychologists said. She had a plan.

"I'm going to sit still and do nothing today," I said fervently. "Mr. Alpert is going to have to drag me from my desk if he wants me to push a button."

I knew I was safe in cooking class. Friday was quiz day, so I didn't have to touch anything but my pencil and the test Dorothy gave us. I'd managed to finish the sketch of a purse that I hoped Mrs. Tottenschott would approve. It wasn't as cool as my first design, but I'd already learned the Academy for Losers had little appreciation for coolness.

The tinny announcement came that first period began in ten minutes; I wolfed down the rest of my cereal and toast. I managed to make it on time, but I had trouble concentrating all day long. Every time I looked at the clock, it would remind me my parents would be here really soon. That reception

Miss Willowood had talked about sounded boring, but being out with my folks tomorrow would be awesome.

"Miss Greene?" I jumped. Mr. Alpert was staring at me. This was not good.

"Yes, sir?"

"Perhaps you'd like to rejoin the class."

Oh, oh, I'd been daydreaming. Delirious visions of hitting the nearest mall with Mom and Dad had occupied the part of my mind that was supposed to be listening to my teacher. I had a suspicion I was going to pay for my lapse.

"As the other students already know, part of our class work is to produce the monthly school newsletter. I was asking for volunteers to type in the various articles." He offered a tight smile. "It might be best for you to take on that task rather than the actual production."

My face warmed, and I knew I was blushing again. A giggle or two came from behind me, which I pretended not to hear. I kept my eyes straight ahead and nodded, forcing myself not to look at the clock again. I really needed to pay attention.

Somehow I got through the rest of the day. I was so excited I didn't eat much dinner, but I wasn't in the mood for mystery meat and veggie surprise anyway. The guys ate everything, but hey, boys have no taste.

It was almost dark before the parents started trickling in. I wanted to press my face against the window like a little kid to watch for them, but I stayed in the activities room like a good girl. The description "activities room" might sound like there's stuff in there like pool tables or video games, but that is so far from the truth it's pathetic. Yeah, there's a big screen TV, but we all have to agree on the show, and whichever teacher's in charge has to agree too. And while I'm all about some Monopoly sometimes, but board games aren't really my thing. Which is unfortunate since there's a whole shelf of them, and we're encouraged to use them.

There is a game system with dance programs and other "good" interactive entertainment, but no one will ever be shooting aliens or busting bad guys in the halls of Hampstead Manor. That would be too much like fun. We "special" kids aren't supposed to have fun. Or so it seems.

"Violet, your parents are here."

I jumped up at the announcement and managed to keep from skipping to the front door to greet them. They looked exactly the way they had when Dad dropped me off three weeks ago, yet it seemed as if it had been years since I'd seen them. Mom wore a big stupid grin and hugged me so hard I thought my ribs would break. Dad hugged me too and pulled something out of his coat pocket as soon as he let me go.

"I wasn't sure if you got this stuff here." He handed me a package of red licorice. I ripped it open right away and offered a long piece to both of them. Dad accepted; Mom said a polite no as she dabbed her eyes with a tissue. I hugged them one more time before starting toward the dining hall, festive on this special occasion. Or so Wendy had told me.

A huge "Welcome Parents" banner hung at the back wall and a long table had been set up at the front with a bright orange tablecloth. A vase full of flowers sat in the middle of it, surrounded by two sheet cakes, bowls of punch and those plastic plates and cups that look like crystal. I wasn't surprised to see Miss Willowood wielding a cake server. I figured anytime there was dessert in this place, she'd be there.

What shocked me was how nice she was when I brought my parents up there. She smiled big at my dad—surprise, surprise—as she gave him an extra-large piece of cake. She also told Mom how pretty her sweater was and how lucky they were to have a daughter like me. I waited for a kicker like "for a non-magical child, that is" but it never happened. As we started toward my usual table, it hit me like a rocket.

Old Wishicould was setting me up. She was being sweet as pie so if I complained to my mom and dad, they'd never believe me. They'd figure I was being whiny and bitchy because I wasn't living at home and hanging with all my friends from Green Hills. Which, of course, meant she'd win.

Like that was going to happen. I decided no word about Miss Willowood or the stupid classes she'd assigned me would cross my lips. So as soon as my mother asked how my classes were going, I changed the subject.

"Please, Mom, don't make me talk about school." I gave her that puppy-dog look I knew she could so not resist. "I want to hear about everything back home. Does Waldo miss me yet?"

The answer to that, I already knew, would be a big no. Waldo was supposedly the family dog but he'd always been like Mom's second child. Whatever genetics created him, they managed to give him fat curls, a squished nose and legs just a little too long for his body. I'd been little when Waldo came to live with us, so he was ancient for a dog. His eyesight had been going for a while and I suspect he's half-deaf, too. But Mom adores him anyway.

That one question launched her into a long recitation of all the endearing things Waldo had done since I'd left. When she finally paused for breath, I knew the answer.

Waldo still didn't realize I existed.

Dad jumped in and commandeered the conversation. I laughed a little too hard at his stories about golfing and his buddies, but I was mucho glad to have him sitting next to me. If I could forget we were in the school dining hall and there were dozens of other families too, it was almost as if we were at our own kitchen table. Almost.

"Hey." I looked up to see Wendy. She was smiling, like always, even though it had to be killing her that we all had our folks here and she didn't. I jumped up and gave her a hug before asking her to join us.

"No, it's okay," she said with a distinct lack of enthusiasm.

"You must sit down and tell us all about yourself," my mother said, patting the chair next to her. "I'm so glad you're Violet's friend."

Sharing my parents seemed kind of weird but it also seemed totally right. Not having them around me all the time had made me realize how lucky I am. I would so hate living a thousand miles away from home and knowing nobody cared if I lived or died. Okay, Wendy's folks would probably be sad if she was dead. And maybe sort of relieved because their little embarrassment had gone away.

By the time we got up to start a tour of the school, the other Terribles had stopped to say hi with their parents in tow. Mom and Dad both seemed happy to know I wasn't spending all my time sitting in my room contemplating suicide.

"Your counselor says you're settling in well." Dad pushed his empty cake plate away. "It's nice to know you're happy with your classes and doing okay."

Dad looked so pleased that I could hardly ruin his weekend by telling the truth. Miss Willowood was a big fat liar. I knew it, she knew it, but I suppose my parents didn't have to know that.

Yet.

"Are we allowed to see your room?" Mom asked, anticipation in her voice.

I nodded. I'd made sure it was spotless, which wasn't too hard since I didn't have much of anything. We went down the hall and up the stairs to my temporary home.

"This is nice." Mom stood in the middle of the room and looked around. "Soothing colors and nothing to distract you from doing your homework. The bedspread is so pretty."

"I see you still have that raggedy bear." Dad nodded toward Alfredo, who was reclining on my pillow.

"And your picture." I led him to the student desk covered by my books. I'd brought my favorite picture of my parents, taken one summer at the town carnival. They looked relaxed, even silly, and seeing it always made me happy. Dad smiled and threw his arm around my shoulders. He didn't say anything, but that was okay. I knew what he was thinking.

Mom fussed a little bit, straightening the corner of the comforter and brushing imaginary dust off the desk. I hadn't thought about this being awkward for them. I mean, it's not like we had that last going away dinner and long lingering goodbyes.

I'd been thinking it was more like taking the family pet to the pound—regrettable but necessary. But with them here in my personal space, which was so unlike my personal space back home, I decided Dad was right. My coming here had been hard on Mom. And him, too, the way he hugged me to his side.

The now-familiar disembodied voice announcing that parents were encouraged to gather in the dining room for a brief overview of Saturday's activities headed off any mushy moments. In other words, it was time for them to leave. I hugged Mom and Dad the hardest ever and made them promise to come back as early as they could. After they left, I grabbed Alfredo and hugged him hard, too. Dad was so wrong. I was never going to give Alfredo up. Not even if I got old and wrinkled and he lost the rest of his fur and the other eye, too.

The hall quieted down fast. I figured everybody else was like me, worn out after hardly sleeping last night and the excitement of seeing our parents. I snuggled down, cradled Alfredo against my neck and went to sleep myself. Tomorrow was going to be a great day.

****

I was outside despite the chilly air when Mom and Dad drove in. Despite my eagerness, I remembered my orders and waited until they reached the sidewalk to join them. Mom looked the happiest she had for a long, long time. Dad looked, well, like Dad always does.

Miss Willowood said hello to Mom and gushed over Dad when we met her on the way to the dining room. The way she smiled at me was like 180 degrees from usual. Once again my folks remarked on how she seemed to like me. And once again I decided not to bust their bubble.

Lunch was fantastic. Brunch, Mom called it. I'm think they brought real cooks in for the occasion because this was nothing like our usual stuff. Croissants with real butter and actual fruit spread, thick and crispy bacon, pancakes as thick as my thumb, and fluffy scrambled eggs were the highlights. At least for me. Mom seemed thrilled with the mixed fruit and the egg white omelets. I think Dad liked the coffee best because he drank at least three cups.

The morning was a bunch of blah, blah, blah. We tagged along on tours of the school, and of course, our parents had the requisite sit-down with teachers. Only parents were allowed in the room so I had no idea what Mr. Alpert said about me. But I took it as a good sign that Mom wasn't bawling again when she came out.

The whole morning was a put on your best face thing. We were shepherded into the auditorium to listen to the choir sing and the orchestra play and a bunch of poetry recited. At least I was safe. I hadn't been there long enough to develop my talents. As if I had any.

The air smelled sweeter when we walked outside after a lunch that was not only edible but quite yummy. It was, I realized, the scent of freedom. For three glorious hours I was no longer an inmate at the Academy for Losers but the one and only daughter of William and Maryanne Greene, about to hit the mall. With Wendy in tow, which made it even better.

I almost felt bad about taking advantage of my parents' guilt. Almost. But I got over it fast as Mom and I set about making my room look less like a cell. Pillows on the bed, a throw rug, a new stuffed rabbit friend of Alfredo and some dopey butterfly decals on the wall gave it a little personality anyway. The butterflies were Dad's idea, but they weren't as bad as I was afraid. And it was the first time I could remember that Dad had done anything but hand me money and tell me to have a good time shopping.

Then the moment I dreaded. The voice of authority announced parental visits were over in five minutes. That was just enough time for me to hug them both hard and walk outside with them. Before I could let the sad creep over me, I felt people on both sides of me linking my arms with theirs. I looked right and saw Wendy and then left to see Muffy. I felt a whole lot lighter inside as the line of cars rolled away. Maybe I could survive this place after all.

Chapter Five

Monday morning. Crap for breakfast. Flat popovers in cooking class, two busted needles in sewing class and three reprimands from Mr. Alpert. Life was back to normal.

Until classes were almost over. When I heard my name over the PA system, I wanted to sink through the floor right there. Everyone looking at me with sympathetic eyes was so not helpful. I was a dead girl walking as I made the long trek down the hall to Miss Willowood's office.

Relief swept over me when I saw Miss Tiddums sitting beside Old Wishicould's desk. She wouldn't let me languish in solitary confinement or whatever the equivalent was here. The reassuring wink she gave helped a lot, too.

Naturally, Miss Willowood had to talk first.

"Transitions are difficult," she said, "and we all understand that. However, it has come to my attention that the problems you are having with your classes may be a factor of inability and not simply adjustment. Despite my reservations, I have been persuaded to modify your curriculum."

Miss Tiddums turned toward me and mouthed, "New classes."

"I have adjusted your electives," Miss Willowood continued, "under light duress. You are being given a two-week probationary period. If your problems persist, we must assume it is you and not the subjects. If that is the case, I'll be speaking to your parents about how to go forward."

Miss Tiddums came to the rescue again, this time talking out loud for us both to hear.

"I'm sure you'll do just fine," she said. "We're here to help you, aren't we?"

I almost laughed at the angelic look she gave Miss Willowood and Miss Willowood's sour scowl back. Now I knew what Miss Tiddums had meant.

I left the guidance office with class transfer papers in hand. Miss Tiddums must have talked to Raz because I was out of food prep and office procedures into, ta da, small engines and horticulture.

I practically danced down the hall and back to my dorm wing. No more exploding flour bags and blizzards of toner. I was supposed to get dirty and make a mess in my new classes.

The Terribles were beyond surprised when they heard my news at dinner.

"Miss Willowood gave you classes you actually wanted?" Oliver shook his head in disbelief. "She never does anything nice for anyone."

"Not for students, you mean," Muffy interrupted. "If she'd been any sweeter to my dad, she would have gone into sugar shock."

That night, before curling up to sleep with Alfredo, I wrote in my journal for the first time since I got here. It took like three seconds because it was only two words: "Yes, hope!"

****

Nervous isn't the word for how I felt walking into engines class for the first time. Scared, maybe. Excited too. Most of all relieved that nobody seemed to care that I was a girl or if I had no idea what I was doing. The guys greeted me with casual waves and "hey" while the teacher directed me to an empty seat.

I knew his name was Mr. Morrison because Raz had told me at breakfast. He'd also told me Mr.

Morrison was probably the coolest teacher ever and I'd fit in, no problem. When he told me that by summer break I could tune up a lawnmower and rebuild a weed whacker, I believed him. Hey, if he thought I could, then I probably could.

Since the others were guys, I figured I was starting at a disadvantage. Turns out I wasn't that far behind most of them. Being non-magical and all, their parents hadn't trusted them with anything that could chop off a toe or maim them for life. I wasn't the only one who didn't know a box-end wrench from a tapper.

"Cheat chart." Mr. Morrison dropped a big laminated card in front of me. One side showed a small engine torn down while the other one had pictures of tools with their names and uses underneath. Mucho helpful, I decided as I studied the diagram.

Trying to keep still as he discussed ignition systems was hard. Having him assign Raz to help me catch up with the rest of the class was fantastic. Mr. Morrison suggested we meet back here in the shop after school ended every day for the next week.

"An hour a day should do it," he said. "I usually stick around until dinner time so I'll be here anyway. You're a smart girl, I can tell, so you should be on the same page as everyone else pretty quick."

I thanked him and took off for English class. The classroom smelled like old shoes and the air freshener sitting on the teacher's desk, so not like the scent of orange cleaner and fuel that hung in the shop. I took my seat, opened my book and waited for the teacher to start telling us, one more time, why good grammar is the most important thing we can learn during our days here.

The girl two chairs over raised her hand. I suppose she has a name, but she's still the blonde at dining table six to me.

"Before we start today," she said, her face the picture of innocence, "could you explain the uses of a colon and a semi-colon again?"

Our teacher was off like a racehorse. The hour flew by as she solved that mystery and rolled on to when the proper use of apostrophes. Way to go, Blondie, I thought in her direction as the period bell rang. Of course, she didn't get the message. So I high-fived her out in the hall and told her good work in there.

My last class was now horticulture. I figured dirt and flowers and all that sort of stuff. I did not figure on our class project being to design a landscape for the west side of the east wing. I was already designing a purse. That should be enough for one non-artistic genius. But there I sat with my pencil and graph paper and a book all about, duh, landscape design. I sneaked a peek at the girl sitting at my left. She was drawing little circles and making boxes. They had to stand for something, but I couldn't figure out what.

I must have looked like a total doofus because the teacher laid a hand on my shoulder and said, "Need a little help, Miss Greene?" She was smiling like she really meant it. Not like Mr. Alpert who sounded snotty no matter what he said to me.

I admitted my total know-nothingness. She came back with a different book. This one actually showed what all those little drawings meant and other important stuff, like how an inch on paper meant a foot of garden. Unfortunately, while I was learning what those marks were for, the other kids had their landscapes all done.

Despair rode on my shoulders as I left the room. I couldn't make it in a magical school. Now I was afraid I couldn't make it in a non-magical one either.

"Cheer up."

I turned to see Mr. Morrison behind me. He was smiling, which made me give a little one back.

"It's going to get better."

"Sure."

"Really. I promise."

Raz was right. Mr. Morrison was more than okay. Maybe I would survive after all.

I followed him back to the shop where a couple of boys were already doing something with tools and a lawn mower engine. So tutor time was a group project.

"Hey." One of the guys nodded as I sat down at the bench next to him with a toolbox.

"Hey. I'm Violet."

"Greg." He started to offer a greasy hand and thought better of it. "Also known as the world's least talented human."

I laughed. "Sorry, I already claim the title."

"I guess we'll have to agree to share it."

While Greg went back to whatever he was doing, I pulled out my tool chart and started matching things up. Before long, I was learning things I never thought I'd need to know, like screwdrivers have different shaped ends and why a spark plug got that name. The hour flew by before I'd memorized them all, but I didn't feel like such a dummy.

"Good job." Mr. Morrison patted my shoulder as I put the toolbox back on the shelf. "I told you that you'd catch on quick."

The glow of his praise stayed with me as I went to the study room to do homework and then on to dinner. After we finished eating, Raz and I went back there so he could help me learn what the other tools were. The science teacher was in charge of making sure we actually studied in the study room, but he was kicked back, feet on the desk, reading a paperback novel with a gruesome cover. So in between identifying sockets and wire clips, Raz filled me in on the kids in the class and Mr. Morrison himself.

"He likes you."

"Uh-huh."

"Seriously. Otherwise you'd be on your own. No after-class stuff, no assigning me to help."

Wow. This was the first time since I'd gotten here that I actually believed I might fit in. I mean except with the Terribles. We were best buds. But the other girls already had their own little cliques, and when one of the boys talked to me, it made me feel weird. I mean, what did we have to talk about except being freaks stuck here together?

When the science teacher's feet hit the floor, Raz started asking me about socket sizes again. By the time the announcement to return to our rooms came, I was beyond ready to retreat to my own little cave. Alfredo sat on my bed and watched as I wrote in my journal for the second night in a row. By the time I finished the rest of my homework, showered and got into bed, I was exhausted. I zonked out the second my head hit the pillow and didn't wake up until that stupid get up voice came in the morning.

****

I so loved my new schedule, especially Mr. Morrison's class. Finally, I'd found something I could do. The guys treated me like, well, just another dude, which was totally cool with me. By the end of the week, I had my own tools paid for by my dad and ordered by Mr. Morrison. I grinned when I opened the package. Every one of them had pink handles.

"I don't think you'll have to worry about the boys 'borrowing' your tools," Mr. Morrison said as he tossed me a roll of pink camouflage duct tape. "You may want to decorate your tool box, too."

I sat cross-legged on my bed that night with my toolbox, tape and scissors. The guys laughed when they saw it the next day. I'd cut out hearts and hammers from the tape and stuck them in a border around the box. Then I'd traced my name on other pieces of tape for the top to make sure everyone knew it was mine.

Learning about how engines work was easy for a geek like me. I love things that make sense, like do this, then that and bingo! Life would be great if everything worked that way.

But it doesn't. Our English teacher is like seriously addicted to Steinbeck, so half our grade for the semester was a big whopping paper we were assigned to write on *The Grapes of Wrath*. I was excited when I thought it some thriller about bioengineered fruit that goes on the rampage. It's all about this family that gets caught in a drought and moves away. So we have to define the theme and discuss character development and other crap nobody cared about.

Half our grade—did I mention that? Before my banishment my parents would have been my partners in this. Mom would take me out for lunch and we'd talk about all that book stuff. Dad would sneak behind her back and buy me the little cheat notes so I could write the paper without actually reading the book.

Deliverance came at breakfast.

"OMG, I know all about that book!" Molly bounced in her seat. "I had to do that in my old school and last semester here. You, me, study room after dinner. We can knock this out in like ten minutes and your little behind is saved."

She settled in her seat. "Then you can save me. I am so lost in Algebra II. Like Hansel and Gretel in the forest lost but without the bread crumbs."

I laughed harder than I should have, but it was so good to know Molly had my back.

****

The day went by without me managing to draw attention to myself, and I was in a very good mood as I walked into the engines lab. A couple of guys waved, but most of them just nodded. I nodded back. Just because I was a girl didn't mean I couldn't do the whole guy thing.

While the other guys did whatever it was Mr. Morrison made them do, I took the tool test. Raz gave me a thumbs up when I walked past him on the way to the teacher's desk to turn it in. I sat back down and chewed on my pencil while I waited to see if I passed or got a big fat red F.

I took a deep breath when Mr. Morrison crooked his finger at me. I knew Miss Willowood was breathing down my neck; if I didn't cut it in here, I'd be back hitting the copier button again. The trek to his desk was like a thousand miles long, especially because he wasn't smiling or anything.

"Very good, Violet." He handed me the paper back. "You missed one or two but definitely an excellent job."

I felt like dancing. I did it. Well, Raz and I did it considering he'd quizzed me for what seemed like forever. I passed the tools test. Now I could start learning about spark plug wires and carburetors and the other stuff that made engines go zoom.

My great mood continued beyond English into horticulture class. Annuals, perennials and wood chip mulch were no match for me. A lot of the houses in our neighborhood had landscapers do their outsides so I closed my eyes and tried to remember what they looked like. Tall stuff in the back, trees on the corners, roses on those wooden things in the back yard—that oughta work for the school lawn, too.

I reported for my hour with Mr. Morrison and spent it reading about how engines work. I could hardly wait to surprise my dad with my brand-new knowledge. Maybe I'd put out a sign next summer offering to fix lawnmowers and save the money toward a car.

There were just a couple of us in after-school today. Greg had his nose in some greasy parts, so Mr. Morrison sat down and talked to me as if I was a real person and not some loser who couldn't cut it in my other classes. Raz was right. He was cool. He said he used to be in the entertainment business, which I figured meant he and his buds had a band when he was in college. I would have asked except Greg dropped the F bomb and Mr. Morrison went over to figure out what the problem was.

****

Dinner sucked even though Oliver chowed down his fish cakes and creamed spinach as though he was starving. The lemon bars for dessert saved me. Wendy gave me hers since she was on a diet once again. That second bar gave me enough energy to tackle that stupid book report.

Molly was a genius. She didn't bring me her papers because that would have been cheating. But whipping through the pages with a highlighter and writing notes in pencil in the margin wasn't. At least I'm pretty sure it wasn't.

Her algebra homework took longer. The left side of Molly's brain must have gone on strike because no matter how much I explained, she couldn't seem to get it. But I'm no quitter. She was going to pass or I'd die trying.

The eagle-eyed, by-the-rules French teacher was on duty tonight, which didn't help at all. Explaining variables and exponents in a whisper to someone who kept whining about how all she wanted to do was eat a peanut butter sandwich and go to bed was the worst thing ever. So I wasn't unhappy when the study hour was over and we went back to our own rooms.

I was still wide-awake by the time I whipped through my homework. I grabbed the box of fancy stationary Mom had brought when they came for parents' weekend and started to write them a letter. It came out as the usual blah, blah, blah because I wasn't sure they knew about my class changes, and I sure didn't want them to find out I traded math tutoring for passing English lit. I was so not ready for my dad to roll all the way up here to give me a lecture on ethics and the value of hard work. I ended my letter with a whole row of XOXO and stuck a stamp on the envelope. Then I curled up with Alfredo and slept the best I had in a week.

Chapter Six

The days whizzed past until it was Saturday
again. The kids who kissed butt got their chance to go
into town for three hours while the rest of us, the
class-changers like me and tardies like Wendy, ate
pizza and played board games for the afternoon. Big
whoop. With a choice of chess, dominoes or
Scrabble, I picked the word game. It ought to take up
the whole time. Maybe if I were stuck with an X, a Q
and a P, I wouldn't have time to resent the ones who
got to leave campus.

I figured I'd never get out without parental
supervision since Miss Willowood makes up the list
of who gets to leave and who has to stay. She made
her token appearance to remind us that with hard
work we too could accompany the school secretary
into the world beyond these walls.

All of us Terribles were left-behinds. Raz and
Oliver had permission to go, but being true and loyal

friends, they stayed with us. So they joined Wendy and me behind the tiles while Muffy and Molly grabbed one of those tower-building games. Every so often we switched places, even though I don't think you're supposed to have a designated speller in Scrabble. But it was more fun that way. When the mini-bus pulled up to disgorge the favored ones, we made sure we were laughing and cutting up as they walked in. Let them wonder what they missed.

To my great surprise, Miss Tiddums saved me from the humdrum dinner experience of Saturday night's tofu lasagna by telling me I was dining with her. I was mucho surprised to see Mr. Morrison at her cottage. They just didn't seem like a couple.

I figured out pretty fast that they weren't. Seems like this evening was all about me.

"Mel says you're quite talented with your hands," Miss Tiddums said. It took me like thirty seconds to realize she was talking about Mr. Morrison.

"I am?" I finally said back.

"My dear Violet, I've been looking for a successor as long as I've been here," Mr. Morrison said.

"A successor?" I hope I didn't look as confused as I felt. "For what?"

"To learn the great secrets of prestidigitation."

"Prestydiggy what?"

"Magic, my dear child. Sleight of hand. Illusions. The very craft that once had crowds on their feet for the Magnificent Morrison."

"What?" My eyes blinked fast. I don't have a bit of magic in me. That's why I was living in loserville.

"There was a time, back before the government testing, when those who possessed natural magic hid their abilities and those of us without any provided great entertainment to the masses." Mr. Morrison sighed. "I'm not saying it was a better time, but it was quite different."

Miss Tiddums interrupted the conversation with her own opinion.

"It was better." Her voice was stern. "There is no excuse for a national system that says one person is acceptable and another is not." Her voice went up a notch. "Why someone with natural magic abilities is considered more suited to be a bank president or physician than someone without I'll never know. Intelligence and determination are what's important."

99

I flinched as bright orange flickers shot out around her. Whoa. Miss Tiddums was throwing sparks. But that couldn't be. Miss Willowood had been insistent that the academy's success was because the faculty was as inept as the students. But if Miss Tiddums' anger looked like road flares, then she had to have magic in her. Didn't she?

I so wanted to ask her about it, but she muttered something about refreshing our tea and hurried to the kitchen. I might not be the smartest person around, but even I knew that was an excuse. She'd lost her cool and her control slipped.

Since Mr. Morrison pretended nothing weird had happened, so did I. He started asking how I liked it at the academy and what I thought of my new schedule. When Miss Tiddums came back with a pot of chamomile tea and the announcement that dinner would be ready in a few minutes, he switched to blah, blah, blah about what an enthusiastic student I was in his class and how I would be fantastic at small engine repairs. I was kind of embarrassed and super happy when a ding came from the kitchen and Miss Tiddums jumped up to get the food.

When Mr. Morrison excused himself to wash his hands, I went to see if I could help her. The wonderful smells got stronger as I neared the stove and my stomach actually grumbled out loud. Miss Tiddums acted as though she hadn't heard it, but I'm think she did. I didn't know if she had magic, but I knew for sure she was one major cook. She'd made chicken and dumplings that looked and smelled just like the ones my gran used to make, which made me even hungrier. I carried the steaming bowl to the table while she brought in buttered corn and creamed peas with tiny potatoes. She made a return trip and came back with fat slices of what I was sure was homemade bread.

If I'd closed my eyes when I took the first bite, I would have thought I was back at my grandmother's for Sunday dinner. The heavenly meal became even better when Miss Tiddums brought a cherry pie with a sugary crust out for dessert. When the ice cream she put on top began to melt as soon as it touched that crust, I knew it was still warm. And yeah, when she asked if I wanted a second slice, I said yes. It was that good.

I figured I'd go back to my room once dinner was over. But Mr. Morrison asked if we could talk a bit more. That stuff about presti whatever was still out there. And before Miss Tiddums walked me back to the main hall, I'd learned tons about what the other kind of magic was all about.

As in he showed me. No clue how he did it, but Mr. Morrison made quarters appear and disappear, made pieces of rope stand up straight and even floated a vase of flowers above Miss Tiddums' coffee table.

"You, Violet, can learn to do that and more." He sat back in his chair and folded his hands across his middle. "I believe you have the ability to outdo me if you stick with it."

So, okay, I could learn to do tricks that might help me pass in the world outside this place. But what he said next sounded mucho shady.

"As you know, the district sponsors a spelling bee each spring," he said. "Every school sends its best students to cast their best spells. Winning is a huge honor.

"Hempstead Manor receives an invitation to participate as a courtesy even though we never have students to compete. It takes magic to cast spells, after all, so we've never gone even once."

He dropped his arms and leaned forward. "You, my dear, can make this the year that

Hempstead Manor not only participates but truly competes."

"This floor has more magic than me," I protested.

"I've reviewed the rules," Miss Tiddums said. "There is no requirement that entrants have a federal magic certification to compete. They simply state that each competitor is required to master a certain act of magic to advance to the next round. The winner is declared after all others fail their assigned demonstration of ability."

Okay, so maybe what they wanted me to do wasn't so sketchy after all. My folks were big on the don't cheat, don't lie thing, but I wouldn't be doing either one. I'd watched the spelling bee the last three years, and I knew the first stuff was simple. Changing water from one color to another, making something disappear, reconnecting a torn sheet of paper—everyone managed those. As the spells got tougher, kids started to drop out. Last year the biggie had been reanimating an electric eel. One of the two finalists managed it; the other one overdid the magic and fried his eel. Which reminded me of my not-so-memorable moment with my dead frog.

"No way can I win this thing," I said.

"We don't expect that." Mr. Morrison hurried to reassure me. "We'll be proud if you get into round two."

Miss Tiddums stood and smiled. "We realize this is a lot to think about. The choice is yours. We wanted to present the opportunity, that's all, and I'd appreciate it if you kept it to yourself. Now we'd better get you back before last bell."

Mr. Morrison left with us but split off for the boys' wing. He was one of the house parents who supervised us. Alas, so was Miss Willowood, who had a small apartment in the main building and roamed the halls all night, or so the Terribles said.

Miss Tiddums walked on to the study area with me; I joined Raz and Wendy at their table for the five minutes until the announcement came to retire to our rooms. They were dying to know why I'd skipped supper. All I told them was that Miss Tiddums took me to her cottage and we talked about my future. Before they could start hitting me with more questions, we had to go our own ways.

I so wanted to talk to Mom and Dad about what Mr. Morrison had suggested, but there was no way I could get anywhere near a phone or a computer. So I did the next best thing. I talked it over with Alfredo as I got ready for bed and even after I slid between the sheets. Okay, I talked and he listened, but his total silence and complete attention let me figure out a lot of stuff. Like whether I was crazy for even considering Mr. Morrison's suggestion.

I dreamed that night, weird as it sounds, about the Magnificent Morrison. Not Mr. Morrison in his Hempstead polo and khakis but like he must have looked back in the day. He was on a big stage with lots of foot lights, wearing a tux and top hat that he ended up pulling a porcupine from. Yeah, porcupine. Like that's going to happen.

His tux was black but he had on a flashy red vest with sequins that sparkled in the lights. A tall blond lady in a tiny outfit did the ta-da thing when the Magnificent Morrison did some magical trick. She had to be a lot braver than me because she climbed in a box and let him cut her in half. Her head was in one part and her feet in the other; when he pulled the halves apart, the crowd went ooh and aah. But they went way past crazy when he pushed the pieces together and she climbed out without even a snag on her little bitty panties.

I woke up with my arms around Alfredo and my heart pounding. Magnificent Morrison shoved the poor girl into a cannon and lit the fuse. I was sure she was going to be shot straight up and get smooshed against the roof. As in dead. Which is why my heart was going whomp-whomp-whomp at like ninety miles an hour.

The alarm clock said it was almost five, but it felt like I'd only been asleep for ten minutes. I unwrapped myself from the sheet, fluffed up my pillow and closed my eyes. And opened them again every ten minutes or so because I was done with sleeping. All I could think of was Mr. Morrison calling me his successor and the evil thought that kept circling through my mind.

If Mr. Morrison was right, I could get through the preliminary rounds if I worked hard enough. And nothing would fry old Mr. Winters more than seeing me up there doing magic after he'd told my folks, what was it, that I needed to be with "others of my kind."

In other words, two steps above a drooling blob.

Naturally, when I did manage to fall asleep, it was right before time to get up. My head was fuzzy and my mouth felt like cotton, but I managed to get dressed and to the dining room on time. I so wanted to tell the Terribles about last night. Wanted to, but remembered how Miss Tiddums had asked me not to blab. I yawned huge and told them I slept super bad. That way if I seemed a little weird they wouldn't be asking questions.

The hours dragged as I managed to make it through class after class. Mr. Morrison treated me like always, which was fine with me. Even Raz didn't notice anything, which was like wonder of wonders because he doesn't miss much. He did see my frustration when I finally got to handle some metal parts.

It sounded super simple. Use a rag and the stuff in the jar and bingo, all the greasy yuck would come off. That was true. What nobody bothered to mention was that the gunk would all migrate to me. And black grease under my fingernails was not the fashion statement I liked to make.

"Use this." Raz handed me a jar of orange cleaner. "It will take all that off."

No surprise, he was right. Once my hands were back to normal, I called to Mr. Morrison to come check my work. It felt so good to hear him say

"Great job" after I'd practically demolished the business machine room all by myself a week ago. When Raz gave me a fist bump on the way past my workbench, my insides got all gushy. I so hoped he didn't see me as just one of the guys now that we were in here together.

****

That night in the study room, I got my answer. Raz sat across from me and pushed a note over. I frowned; this better be important because we could both end up with demerits. I pulled it into my book and opened it. I know my eyes must have gotten big because he started to grin.

"March mid-semester dance with me?"

I nodded, knowing I had to be grinning too. Wendy and Muffy had told me all about the mid-semester dance. Kids who went to Hempstead couldn't date each other, and dates from outside the academy were forbidden. That meant everybody went alone. In theory anyway. Some people paired up anyway even though the consequences were, as Muffy said in a mysterious tone, "super, super dire."

And Raz was willing to risk them for me. I sighed. I mean, how romantic was this?

I scribbled, "yes, yes, yes!" on the bottom of the note and slid it back to him. My mind was reeling. I was going to break the rules. Me, Violet Greene, who returned paper clips to teachers if they dropped them by my desk. I'd chase the mailman a block if he left someone else's junk mail at our house. I was going to have a real, actual date with the coolest guy I'd ever met.

I figured everyone could see the excitement bubbling out of me, but I tried to chillax even though I was two seconds away from a happy dance. My bubble deflated fast when the ogre at the desk, er, Miss Willowood, motioned me to her with a big frown on her face. I took a deep breath and pushed back from the table. She'd seen the note passing. She'd call my folks. I was doomed.

"Yes, ma'am?" I asked when I got there, using all my manners. I hoped for the best but expected the worst.

I was pleasantly surprised. Instead of tapping her fingers on the desktop and fixing me with that "I'm the boss" stare, she smiled at me. Or maybe she was holding back gas. Whatever.

"Mr. Morrison tells me that you show amazing aptitude in his class."

Whoa. I didn't know what to say, so I kept my mouth shut and nodded.

"He also requested that he be allowed to tutor you for a few weeks to ensure you catch up with the others." She paused and steepled her fingers. "Granting such a request is highly unusual. I have discussed it with Miss Kalazmenthian who will be sitting in to monitor your progress."

Who the heck was Miss Kalazmenthian? I frantically searched through my brain trying to figure it out but came up with absolutely nothing.

"Miss Tiddums as she refers to herself." Now Old Wishicould looked like she'd been sucking on a lemon. "She seems to think you two are forming a bond beyond her role as school psychologist."

"If Mr. Morrison thinks I need help, I wouldn't want to turn it down. And it will be all right if Miss Tid, I mean, Miss Kalazmenthian joins us."

"Very well then." Miss Willowood unfolded her fingers and gave a little nod. "Each evening for the final hour of study. Is that acceptable to you?"

Acceptable? It was a gift tossed down from the angels. A whole hour of not being here was like the hugest gift ever. But I played it cool. I nodded and said, "Okay."

My journal found out how excited I was that night and so did Alfredo as I snuggled him against me and went to sleep earlier than usual. Maybe this place had potential after all.

****

"Miss Greene?" The soccer coach was in charge of the study room again tonight. She was green at this, I guess, because she actually came over to tap my shoulder as I tried to figure out why any parent would name a boy Connie and give a girl a name like Rose of Sharon. I mean, what's wrong with Jarod and Kayla anyway?

When she whispered, "You can be excused now," I nodded, grabbed my books and took off with a wave to the Terribles.

Miss Tiddums was waiting in the hall. We chatted about the vile food at dinner on the short walk to the shop room where Mr. Morrison was waiting. I was confused. The shop was neat and he had on a white polo shirt instead of his usual grease-won't-show navy one. When he offered me the forbidden, a can of cola and a package of my fave snack cakes, I knew something was up.

"Have you considered my proposal?" he asked as he popped the top on his own can of cola.

111

"Would Miss Willowood approve?" I asked in return.

He laughed. "Most definitely not."

"Then I'm in." I clinked cans with the two of them and waited to hear what came next. It turned out to be awesome magic that looked totally natural to me but they said were just tricks. Like breaking a toothpick into pieces and putting it back together. And drinking a glass of water but then the water came right back.

"Cool," I breathed as Mr. Morrison made the rope dance again and then made it stand straight up.

"So simple a child could do it," he said with a smile. "Or a teenage girl who is competing in this year's spelling bee."

I promised Mr. Morrison not to tell anyone how he, and now me, did these things. And yeah, I was slow and clumsy at first. As in, at one point I tossed the rope back to him and told him he had the wrong girl.

"Maybe you have to possess a little bit of magic to do that stuff, Mr. Morrison." I was trying hard not to cry. "We've proved I don't have even a tiny bit."

"It takes time, Violet." His voice was calm, like when Mom talked to Waldo after he did something stupid. "And while we're together like this, please call me Morry."

"You can call me Bit." Miss Tiddums smiled widely. "I'm an only child so I carry every family name you can imagine. The whole thing barely fit on my birth certificate: Elizabeth Virginia Coldwell Nicholas Tiddums Kalazmenthian. From the time I came home from the hospital, though, everyone called me Bit. Because I was a preemie, I guess."

Okay, I totally got that. Miss Tiddums was still little with tons of personality packed in. Even if she did pick brains for a living.

Miss Tiddums—Bit—leaned forward. "Because I had no siblings, my family had great expectations for me. They had my life charted out. If I'd followed their path, I'd be the wife of a senator or maybe even the president. I'd host dinners and charm people at the country club. I certainly wouldn't have followed my passion for working with children who are following paths of their own."

So that's why I liked her so much. She'd been a disappointment to her parents, too.

"Do I have to call you Bit?" I asked. "I think I like you as Miss Tiddums better."

She laughed. "You can call me anything but late to dinner."

That was so something my dad would say that I had to laugh too. The break was good because I tried the rope thing again and yes, it stood straight up. Miss Tiddums clapped her hands like I'd just parted an ocean. That felt good.

The hour went by fast. So fast that I couldn't believe it when Morry patted my back and said, "You're doing great. See you in class tomorrow."

Small engines and sleight of hand…this place was getting way better than I could ever have imagined.

Chapter Seven

"I'm glad you called me, Miss Willowood."

"Oh, please, call me Lydia."

"Only if you drop the Mr. Winters and use Al."

"Agreed."

Alfred Winters leaned back in his chair and listened to Lydia's story. He knew her, of course; everyone in the district knew each other from training sessions and mandatory meetings. But he hadn't realized what a good spy she could be until right now. If what she said was true, his entire career was in jeopardy. If he'd transferred a student with abilities into a vocational education program, the district chairman of assessments would have his head. His charge at this school was to foster the innate magic of every child, no matter how small an amount it might be.

Could he have missed something with that Greene girl?

"The monthly report I received said she was doing well in academic subjects but doing poorly in her other classes," he said. "Was that wrong?"

"Oh, no. She can't make a single copy without blowing up the machine, and Violet practically wrecked the student kitchen. But the moment she gets near a lawnmower engine, she excels. It's simply not possible."

"Perhaps she's getting help," Al suggested.

"No, no. Mr. Morrison has her in after-class tutoring but only to bring her up to date with the other students. According to her classmates, she excels."

"Hmmm." Al knew why Lydia was suspicious. The girl's dexterity hadn't been an issue here because she'd had all college prep classes, but it sounded like she'd been succeeding gloriously at Hempstead. In all his years as a teacher and then an administrator, he'd never met a child who could transform overnight. Yet that seemed to be the case with Violet Greene.

"You're certain no one is doing her work for her," he suggested again.

116

"Impossible. I've observed that classroom more than once. Each student has his own workstation and Mr. Morrison is constantly supervising. I believe that for some reason she hid her abilities at your school and is using them to cheat at ours."

Al closed his eyes and tried to think. Total humiliation would be his if he brought the girl back and she did as poorly as she had in the past. But he'd get the same result if he allowed her to stay at the training school and the district chairman found out she'd been magical all along. Granted, she'd failed dismally on the national tests and her teachers had signed off on her transfer. Was she just a garden-variety troublemaker?

"Keep an eye on her," he finally said. "Discreetly. We will get to the bottom of this, trust me."

Al hung up and stared at the wall without really seeing it. He was good at his job. He had the evaluations and awards to prove it. The district chairman of assessments was retiring next year, and Al wanted that job. He'd like to finish out his career bossing around the principals and blasting them for poor test results. The law was clear. Students

117

deficient in magic as proven by the national tests went into alternative training, weeded out before they reached high school, thank goodness. But every so often one slipped through.

Like the Greene girl.

He shoved back his chair, walked into the outer office and told the secretary he was leaving for the day. He needed to get away from here for a while, give the problem some thought. He couldn't think of a better place to do that than out at the range, mentally propelling golf balls at teeny, tiny, teenage girl targets.

****

"My, my, my." Lydia Willowood sighed and stood, stretching her arms above her head. The mighty Alfred Winters was worried. The edge in his voice had betrayed him. The man was vain; he based his whole life on always being right. But it appeared as if he might have been wrong this time.

Unless someone was helping Violet cheat. She reached into the file cabinet behind her and pulled out the file on Mr. Morrison's small engine class. She pictured the boys in her mind as she scanned the list of names and stopped at Razland's. Those two sat at the same dining table, and she'd seen them studying together. She tapped the paper with a long fingernail. This might well be the source of Violet's sudden excellence.

Perhaps they both needed to visit Miss Kalazmenthian. Separately of course. Children in adolescence often had a false sense of loyalty. Perhaps a little time with the school psychologist might help them put their values in perspective. And if that failed, she'd take care of it herself. She refused to be the laughing stock of the district, the counselor who guided a perfectly good student into a less than ordinary life.

Stalking from her office, she headed toward Mr. Morrison's classroom. He was such a sweet man and so dedicated to helping his students reach their full potential. He would be as horrified as she was to find cheaters in his class. Maybe she should make surprise visits from time to time to help him figure things out. And she ought to invite him to dinner some evening. After all, the poor man was single, living in the boys' wing. He deserved a home-cooked meal if anyone did.

****

I knew something was up when Miss Willowood walked into the room. Everybody knew she didn't leave her office any more than she had to. For her to go up a flight of steps and walk down the long hall required some sort of emergency. I figured it must have something to do with me when Miss Willowood pulled my teacher aside and then glanced in my direction.

My heart began to pound. Everyone knew when that happened, it meant one of two things. Either I was in big trouble or something was wrong at home. All sorts of terrible thoughts filled my mind. Maybe my dad had a heart attack. Or my mother had been in a horrible car accident and was in a coma. Or dead. A terrible image popped into my head of our house on fire with Mom standing on the neighbor's yard screaming for Waldo and Dad heroically dashing into the flames to save the stupid dog.

When Mr. Morrison tipped his head in a "come here" motion, I took a deep breath and prepared myself for the worst. Miss Willowood had her arms folded across her ample middle and she looked stern. Or sad. Maybe depressed. It was hard to tell; her facial expressions were limited.

Everybody watched me go. Raz seemed worried. I began to wonder if he knew something I didn't. Like maybe the curriculum gurus had decided girls had no business learning about spark plugs and intakes. Dread filled me at the thought of having to go back into that stupid office machines class.

I was mucho sure that was it when Mr. Morrison left everybody working alone while he and Miss Willowood took me into the classroom. Yeah, there was a big glass window between the classroom and the shop, but he never watched from there. He was always with us. Always.

"Is there something you'd like to tell us?" Miss Willowood asked in the voice of doom. I expected her to pull out a tazer or something..

"No." My voice squeaked, much to my dismay. I cleared my throat and tried again. "I don't know what you mean."

"I understand you're doing quite well in this class despite your lack of experience and being a girl."

So there it was. Old Wishicould was going to yank me out of the only class I really liked because I didn't have dangly parts. I risked a glance at Mr. Morrison who mouthed "Relax" at me.

"I feel an affinity with machines," I replied, ripping off a sentence I'd heard in a bad sci-fi movie.

"She does." Mr. Morrison had my back.

"Would either of you be opposed to my sitting in from time to time?"

We both shook our heads. Miss Willowood fixed me with one of her "I'm watching you" stares as she left the room. My legs trembled as I walked back to the carburetor I was supposed to be taking apart so I could put it back together on Monday. The guys looked at me with worried faces but I gave a thumbs up. Later I'd tell Raz; nobody else needed the details.

I so wanted to tell him at dinner, but I didn't want the other Terribles to know. Wendy already detested Miss Willowood. I could see her sticking a glob of peanut butter in the woman's desk drawer in revenge. And Muffy was a creature of impulse. She was as likely to confront Miss Willowood in the hall as keep my secret.

The study room was only half-full tonight. I learned why when Molly slid into the seat next to me.

"Where is everybody?" I asked in a low voice.

"TV room. There's some stupid game that the boys wanted to see, so they opened it. I figure the coach was behind it."

I hid my disappointment. Raz loved basketball, and if it was such an important game that the TV could be on during a school night, that's where he'd stay until it was over. Maybe I could waylay him in the morning before breakfast.

I so missed my phone. It would only take like ten seconds to text him my news, but I had to plot and plan instead.

"Are you studying, dear?" I looked up to see Miss Willowood looking down at my closed notebook.

"Uh, thinking about a term paper," I fibbed.

"Perhaps you should read your book instead."

Doomed to read about the traveling Joads, I found where I'd left off the night before as Miss Willowood watched for what seemed like hours. Once she waddled to the teacher's desk, Molly leaned over and whispered, "What did you do to tick her off?"

I shrugged. "My mere existence irritates her."

Molly laughed loud enough to gain a scowl, but Miss Willowood kept her butt in the chair. I wanted to tell Molly the whole story, even how I was going to take part in the spelling bee, but I was saved from blabbing by Mr. Morrison's appearance in the

123

doorway. I said a hasty goodbye, grabbed my stuff and hurried to meet him. Miss Tiddums was already in the shop waiting for us.

I did better tonight. Morry high-fived me and Miss Tiddums set out some frosted pumpkin whole grain cupcakes that tasted lots better than they sounded. She said we were celebrating, but I think she just likes to make stuff.

Until Morry said, "We'll work on that Monday," I forgot for a while that it was Friday. I'd gotten enough good girl points to attend the movie party the next afternoon. It was my first one, natch, but the Terribles told me it wasn't as lame as it could be. Two movies, pizza and popcorn and an afternoon not spent trying to find something to do sounded good to me. Especially since all six of us were going to be there, which was awesome.

Fridays were snack nights. Tonight when we got to the dining room there were homemade cookies and cups of chocolate milk, two of my most favorite things ever. Since there were lots of cookies, I took three. This super-secret stuff made me hungry.

Stuffed but happy, I walked up to our rooms with Wendy. She yakked the whole way about how she heard how tomorrow's films were her very fave vampire movies and how super buttery the popcorn was. I completely forgot Miss Willowood's weirdness by the time I got ready for bed and snuggled under the covers. This had been the absolute best week since I got here. Better yet I had a super sneaky date to get ready for even if I did have to wait almost a whole month until the dance.

****

"So what team are you on?" Molly settled into the chair beside mine.

I was majorly impressed. The staff had made the TV room look like a movie theater. The mini-sofas and soft chairs sat into rows and a popcorn machine made the place smell like the real thing. I tried to count how many were there and came up with twenty-two. The old-timers here had boarded the bus for the mall or the movie theater, and some kids didn't have enough points even to come in here. I realized as I looked around I knew everyone's name. And they all knew mine.

"I don't know for sure," I said to Molly. "Vampire probably."

"You've got to be kidding." She started trying to persuade me to line up behind the hot werewolf guy. Her hands flew as she talked, and I thought she might bounce right out of her chair before she was done. I gave up and joined her in werewolf adoration mostly to make sure she didn't wind up on her butt.

Even though I'd seen both movies before, I cheered and gasped and peeked through my hands like everybody else. Back home I went to the movies all the time with my friends, but I don't think I ever had as much fun as I did that day. Plus it was what I needed to forget about all the stress of the last week and the never-ending attention of our less than beloved guidance counselor.

A bunch of teachers watched the movie with us including Miss Tiddums who cheered for the good vampires as loud as anyone else. Which made me wonder again why nobody had married her yet. She's smart, she's funny and her food was fantastic. I'm sure it wasn't because she loved her last name.

Mr. Morrison wasn't there. He probably went with the mall kids or maybe he was sitting in a brand-new movie with some of the boys. I thought about what he was teaching me for like a minute before the pizza arrived and I got in line for pepperoni and onion, the best kind ever. Two slices later I was ready for more vampire action.

Dinner was more disappointing than ever after the afternoon's junk food. Ollie eats anything, so he was the only one to clean his plate of the mystery meat loaf, creamed onions and corn soufflé. Butterscotch pudding was dessert, and he ate his own, Molly's and Wendy's before he announced he was full.

Since there's no study time on Saturday, a bunch of us started playing board games. I picked Parcheesi. I beat my mom and dad in it all the time. Or they let me win. Whatever.

We kept switching around playing against each other until the "retire to your rooms" announcement came. I couldn't believe it was ten o'clock already. This had been one majorly fast day.

Miss Tiddums surprised me by asking if I'd mind showing her my room. For one teeny second I wondered if she was going to search my stuff, but then I reminded myself who was asking. She had something else in mind. I found out what once the door almost closed behind us, open the mandatory two inches because I wasn't alone.

Shock of all shocks, it had nothing to do with learning to make a bouquet of flowers disappear.

127

"I've been told to schedule tests for you and your friend Razland," she said. "I'm not sure why, so I'm doing a little sleuthing. Have you two been up to something that can get you in trouble?"

I dropped down on my bed. Miss Willowood was doing this. No way could it be random, not after her coming around to snoop like she did yesterday. I didn't need Miss Tiddums to remind me to keep my extra-curricular homework hush-hush.

Filling her in on Miss Willowood's visit seemed like a good idea so I did. Turns out she knew; Mr. Morrison had already told her. She said good night and see you in chapel as she left the room, but I could tell the wheels in her head were turning. I'm figured she'd have the results of my test even before I take it.

Chapter Eight

February has to be the most boring month
ever. Even though it's the shortest one, it's so super
long. Having Miss Willowood coming into my
classes didn't help. Yeah, she started dropping by to
see what I was doing in horticulture, too. I wondered
if my folks would believe me if I told them how
paranoid she was. Just because I was getting As in
both classes didn't mean she had to keep me under
surveillance like I was a criminal.

"Maybe I should be a landscaper," I said at
the red-food dinner the cooks fixed for Valentine's
Day. For once they did a good job. Ollie wasn't the
only one to chow down his tomato soup, cherry-
covered chicken, red gelatin salad and strawberries
with bright pink whipped cream.

"Maybe you should decide what you're going to do with your folks." Wendy wiggled her fork at me. "Or have you forgotten that it's almost parents' weekend again?"

"Nooo." I strung the word out because I almost had. There was too much in my life for me to remember everything all the time. And that was almost two weeks from now.

"Unless you screw up big time between now and then, you get to spend the day with them...away from here."

I knew that, but hearing Wendy say it out loud made it real. Freedom was mine! Well, for a few hours anyway. But I'd take every moment outside these boring walls.

There wasn't much the Terribles didn't tell me, but they had hidden one surprise. Instead of the announcement that the dinner hour was over, the announcement came to remain in our seats. I was shocked when the teachers began carrying stuff in. I almost cried when Mr. Alpert handed me a heart-shaped box of chocolates with a little box on top and a ribbon tied around them both. I read the card attached: "Happy Valentine's Day from Mom, Dad and Waldo" and smiled

Other kids were getting gifts from their families, too. Even Wendy got a big balloon, which made her grin like I'd never seen before.

I know my eyes got huge when I opened the little box. Inside it I found a silver locket on a thin chain. Inside, my mom's picture was on one side and my dad's on the other. It took me like five seconds to get it out of that box and around my neck. I couldn't even feel the chain, it was that tiny, but the locket was a cold spot against my skin that warmed up quickly. The stupid thought went through my head that it was because their love was leaking out.

We took our gifts to our rooms before we came down for study time. Which, as it turned out, wasn't study time tonight. The art teacher had set up craft stations for all of us, and we used the time to make fancy valentines to give our parents when they came at the end of the month.

Mom's was as pretty as I could make it with lace and stick-on hearts. Dad's was silly because he likes goofy stuff. I drew on UFOs and cute little aliens. Wendy was a lot more enthusiastic than I expected, probably because of the balloon. I noticed that the art teacher gave her a big red envelope to decorate, which was good. Somebody would make sure her card went to Colorado. That made me happy too.

I barely got done before the five-minute warning. I headed upstairs with my special cards and a sudden longing to hug my parents really tight.

****

The next day was back to normal. I hadn't even gotten through the breakfast line before Miss Willowood came up and told me to go to see Miss Tiddums instead of going to my first class. Not like I was shocked since I knew the plan. It's the way she smirked, like she knew something I didn't.

The last person I expected to see in Miss Tiddums' room was Raz. No way would old Wishicould let us do this thing together. A twinkle in Miss Tiddums' eye as she said hello made me think that maybe she was breaking the rules. Again.

Until she asked, "Why did you ask me to let you into the library that night?"

Busted. I managed not to look at Raz, but I bet he looked as guilty as I felt. Taking a deep breath, I told the truth.

"So I could talk to Raz."

"I'm assuming you had a good reason."

"I had to." The words came rushing out. "I got stupider by the minute in the classes Miss Willowood stuck me in, and I ran into Raz and he always knows what to do and…"

"Okay already." Miss Tiddums held up her hand to stop me. "That's what I figured since Raz joined you."

"You knew he was there?"

"Violet, I've been at this school for fifteen years, and you don't want to know how many kids I worked with before I arrived here. Hiding things from me is not easy."

Relief flooded through me. Not only had she known why I wanted to go to the library, she believed my answer. Mr. Winters would have been calling my parents and telling him what a bad influence I was on so-called normal kids, the ones who can hide their screw-ups with the wave of a hand.

Buoyed by that relief, I revealed my only remaining secret. I told her Raz asked me to be his date for next month's dance. I thought Raz might be mad, but he looked happy. Maybe he felt like me: Telling somebody made it real. Telling someone made it official. Raz liked me, and I liked him.

133

I waited for the inevitable scolding. Instead Miss Tiddums explained to Raz how he could buy me a wrist corsage without anyone knowing it came from him and advised me to make sure I danced with another boy or two so it didn't look like we were exclusive.

"Ollie and Greg," Raz said right away. "Most of the guys need a cattle prod to dance with a girl."

All three of us laughed. Then Miss Tiddums got down to business. Her face got all serious.

"I need to ensure that you're not helping Violet too much with her engine class," she said to Raz. "Neither of you are being accused of cheating; I think you know better than that. We simply want to make certain that Violet does everything on her own to get the full benefit of her training."

Whoa, those last words sounded like she was channeling Miss Willowood.

"She was doing things on her own, correct?"

Raz was careful how he answered, so I figured he caught the hint, too. She asked me the same kind of question, only asked differently. She listened to both of us before nodding her head in one sharp movement. We just sat there as she made notes in what I figured were our permanent files. We didn't even look at each other. No way was I doing anything to mess up my going to the mid-March dance. I'm sure Raz felt the same way.

We parted outside Miss Tiddums' office. He went to the last few minutes of his first period class, and I went to mine. I so wanted to ask him what that was all about, but we didn't have time.

I had a hard time concentrating the rest of the day. What had Miss Tiddums written in our folders? I trusted her not to tell about our plans for the dance, but who knew what else she put in there?

Raz was already in Mr. Morrison's class when I got there. He gave me a hey-there nod and went back to talking to Greg and some guy whose name I still hadn't learned. Me, I did the same thing. Today was classroom day, so I stashed my other books and sat down in one of the unoccupied seats. Raz and Greg ended up sitting right beside me, one on the left and one on the right. And they kept talking across me until Mr. Morrison called for order. But Greg winked at me before we opened our books, so I figured Raz had clued him in about the dance and how he was supposed to spend some time with me.

Learning stuff wasn't nearly as much fun as doing stuff, so I was glad when the bell rang. Raz bumped my hip with his on the way out and grinned before we headed to our final classes.

I seriously did not know that dirt wasn't, well, just dirt until I started in the horticulture class. Today we mixed stuff in to make it right for this kind of plant or that one, which made the time go fast for a science geek like me. Miss Willowood may think my college prep classes at Green Hills were stupid, but hey, that chemistry class was making me shine like a rock star today.

My mood was great all through the after class/before dinner social time and at dinner too. We had pork chops, one of the few foods I could recognize even with a thick layer of gravy on top. I was excited to see the mashed potatoes because here we get the real thing, made from actual potatoes and not mixed up from a box. The apple crumb cake for dessert made me wonder if we were all dying tonight because if I were condemned, I'd take this meal as my last one.

A wave of disappointment swept over me when I went to the study room and found Mr. Morrison behind the desk. That meant no magic lessons tonight, and over the weekend, I'd figured out how to get that rope to dance like a worm. He winked when I walked in, though, so I should have known he had something up his sleeve.

"See you in the morning," he said casual like as I left the room after the announcement that study time was over. "I'll be in my room at seven."

Since fifty-nine other people were leaving at the same time, I couldn't ask questions. I figured I'd just go there before breakfast and see what was up. So imagine my surprise when I got back to my room and found a letter under my door. I recognized Miss Tiddums' handwriting instantly.

"Powwow in Morry's classroom before breakfast," was all it said. I decided I should rip the note up and throw away the pieces; I've seen my share of spy movies. If I'd had matches and a place to do it, I would have burned it even.

I was wide-awake when I went to bed, sure I'd never go to sleep. Naturally, I was wrong. I fell asleep right away. I woke up a little bit before the 6:30 get-up announcement and hurried down to the bathroom. I wanted to slip away before the rest of the girls came out of their rooms. Much as I loved Wendy, Molly and Muffy, I knew they'd demand to know where I was going and why. I didn't intend to tell the first part, and I had no idea about the second.

The usual grease and gasoline smell of the engine lab had a new scent added in. It took a second until I realized it smelled like oranges and cinnamon. I wasn't surprised when Miss Tiddums popped out of the classroom to offer me a fresh-baked muffin. I took a bite and sighed. If heaven had a taste, this was it. I'd have to make my appearance in the dining room in fifteen minutes, but no way could anything there compare with this.

Morry only took a few seconds to drop the news.

"We're going to have to cancel our evening sessions."

I stared at him in dismay. I'd gone from not wanting any part of this illusions stuff to getting excited about going to the spelling bee. It wasn't fair.

I told him so. Miss Tiddums held up a finger to shush me and said, "Miss Willowood's concerns only change our plans, not cancel them. I've arranged for an alternative."

I had no clue how sneaky teachers could be until now. Morry and Miss Tiddums had cooked up a plan to actually get me away from Hempstead for my special learning experiment.

"Miss Willowood asked for additional tests, and I provided them," she said. "My evaluation yesterday was that it would be good for you to have off-campus vocational experiences since your previous academics had been directed toward college. Since that's been done before, she could hardly object."

Whoa. I was going to keep on learning from Morry and do it away from these white walls and brown floors? Maybe I was hallucinating.

The plan was so simple. Three days a week, right after horticulture class, Mr. Morrison would take me to a repair shop run by a friend of his. I'd spend a half-hour working there, and then Morry the magician would spend an hour in the guy's parts room teaching me the stuff I really wanted to learn.

Miss Tiddums leaned toward me.

"You're taking a chance," she said. "Miss Willowood will check with the shop owner, of course, so you need to do your best. If she thinks it's not helping, then she'll cancel permission."

I'm smart enough to figure out what she meant. If this didn't work, Hampstead wouldn't be in the spelling bee for the first time and I would be just another nothing-special kid. I would be the world's best assistant whatever ever.

****

"You get to leave school?" Wendy was beyond impressed when I finally told the Terribles at dinner. "For real?"

I nodded. Ollie jumped in before I could say anything more.

"You're not the first." He pointed his butter-covered knife at me. "You know they do that so when you screw up, they can say I told you so."

"Then I won't screw up." I popped a cherry tomato from my salad into my mouth and waited for someone to change the subject. That happened before I could even swallow. Muffy began talking about the soufflés they made in cooking class that day, which made me even more grateful I'd escaped it. If I couldn't break eggs and flip 'em for an omelet, a soufflé was way out of my league.

"It sucks that you have to miss free time," Raz said. I know he meant it sucked that I couldn't spend it with my friends. Hempstead was like the military. Every minute was planned except for the precious ninety between the end of the last class and dinner. Not like we got to do much except hang out, but that was enough. The Terribles said that when the weather was warm we could go out and sling Frisbees and stuff. But by then maybe I'd know everything I had to for the spelling bee. I hoped.

Everybody started talking about parents' weekend and mid-semester grades. Funny how I didn't even think about my grades much here. It's not like I was competing for a scholarship at a big name school or worried about embarrassing my parents. By now everyone at home already knew their only child was a certified loser. How much worse could I make it for them?

****

"Good evening, Al."

Al Winters winced at the flirtatiousness in Lydia's voice. Their arrangement was strictly business. He hoped she realized that. The only future he and Lydia Willowood had together was making sure Hempstead Academy was not fostering a slacker too lazy to use her abilities.

"I assume you have an update."

"Oh, yes. Unless you'd like me to call you for another reason."

"No, no. Please fill me in."

After he hung up, Al tried to decide if the information had been important enough for him to delay his dinner to take Lydia's call. The Greene girl had caught up so fast she didn't need tutoring even though she'd barely joined the class. Instead, the instructor was escorting her to a shop in town so she could get the hands-on experience she needed after missing the first semester. That certainly sounded like a responsible teacher attempting to offer a top-notch education experience to every student.

Then again, that co-op experience could be a smoke screen hiding something unsavory. If that girl had even a tiny bit of magic, she might be able to enhance her ability enough to force a transfer back to his school. And that humiliation would destroy any chances of a promotion. He toyed with his necktie. If he could find the time, he might take a little ride down the road and check things out for himself.

He sighed. As if he could find time for anything but his responsibilities. He opened his briefcase and pulled out the latest set of test results. Green Hills always led the district. If even one student appeared to be doing less than his best, the teachers had better be ready for heads to roll.

Al was halfway through the sheaf of printouts when he gave in to the driving impulse to check out Violet's past performance. Packing the test results back into his briefcase, he took them with him as he walked briskly to his car and headed back to the school. A quick trip through a drive through would have to do instead of the leisurely meal he had in mind. The best way to handle a crisis was to keep it from happening.

He was pleased to see that his secretary had left her computer on. He quickly found the results from last year's magic abilities testing and pulled up Violet's results.

Lydia Willowood had to be wrong. He studied the numbers again. Only her academic skills had kept the girl in Green Hills. She didn't have enough natural magic to move a pen from one side of a table to another.

He closed the file and gave a contented sigh. Let Hempstead have her. She was no threat.

Chapter Nine

The shop was small but neat. Everything in it was old but in a good way. The place reminded me of my grandpa's basement with jars of screws and bolts and tools hanging off pegboard racks on the wall. The owner, whose work shirt had a patch that read Franklin, introduced himself as Snick. I figured out why when he offered me a Snickers bar from a stash under the counter where the old-fashioned cash register sat.

While the men talked, I looked around the room. The portable phone sitting on the counter was a plus. The lack of any other electronics was a definite negative. Snick didn't even have a TV on the wall. This must have been like when my parents were my age when video games were sucky and nobody had even invented the Internet yet. If this were a movie, I'd be in a time warp where everything I knew was still in the future.

But this was my life here in the twenty-first century. The cell phone hanging off Morry's belt was proof of that.

"Come on back and let me show you how to take apart a weed whacker." Snick waved his hand for me to follow him. "We'll let the professor here watch the front."

Whoa. Everything missing in the customer part of the store was back here. A computer and printer sat on a beat-up desk in a corner. Shelves next to them held power drills and other tools. Snick pointed toward a mini-frig and said, "You get thirsty, go look in there."

It didn't take me long to figure out that Snick's a man of few words. "Watch me" was the bulk of his conversation. He grabbed a cordless screwdriver and undid some screws, and things started coming off on the weed whacker. I was surprised how quickly time went by. It seemed like we'd just started when Morry came in to see how we were doing.

"We'll let her set until tomorrow." Snick leaned back against a tool bench. "You two have your work to do now."

Morry unzipped a backpack he must have brought in while I was back here with Snick. He did some amazing stuff again before he sat back to watch me. Tonight the rope was perfect. It stood up straight, it danced, it even went back into one piece again after I cut it in two.

"Great job." He patted my shoulder and put his stuff away. "You're doing really well."

"Good enough to represent Hempstead?"

"That's up to you." His face was serious. "I can teach you the skills, but I can't make you a magician. That comes from deep inside. Not only do you need confidence in what you do, you need to be an artist. Every movement has to be smooth and eye-catching. When you're on stage, you're giving the audience a gift. You're lifting them out of their everyday life into something special, something truly memorable."

He wasn't talking to me anymore. His gaze was far beyond the walls of this shop. The look on his face let me know how much he missed that world of make-believe and how he wanted to share it.

146

"Whatever it takes, I'll do it," I said. "I promise. Cross my heart."

"Friday is the deadline to submit names for this year's spelling bee." Morry's eyes fixed on my face.

"Send mine in." A flood of excitement rolled over me. "I can get up early to practice and stay up late, too. You can trust me."

Morry stuck his hand out and we shook on it. That's when I knew I had to do this and do it right. My dad always said that a man's handshake is as good as his word. That applies to girls, too, I guess.

We got back with just enough time for me to clean up for dinner. The Terribles were already at the table when I slid into my chair. Like two seconds later, the first table started through the line. I could hardly wait it was us. I was starving. Hungry enough not to care if it was cod fish and fried cabbage night. The banana pudding for dessert was super special; I was the first one to say yes when Muffy asked if anyone wanted hers.

I needed study time because the outline of my book review was due the next day, and I still hadn't finished reading the book. I slogged through it until it was time to go back to our rooms and kept reading until I finally finished. My last thought before everything went black was that I was going to be one tired puppy in the morning.

And I was. I dragged myself up, showered and yawned my way down the hall. Lucky for me there were no pop quizzes or discussions in my classes, so nobody seemed to notice I was only half there. Engine class was all about throttles, and in landscape class all we did was plant vegetable seeds into peat trays. Part of our curriculum was to raise bedding plants to sell to the staff and community. This first step was super easy.

Raz and Molly found me when free time began. They wanted to know what happened the afternoon before at Snick's shop. I told them all about the place and how I was helping to fix a weed whacker, but I didn't say a word about what Morry was teaching me. He and Miss Tiddums were depending on me to keep the secret.

"So are you getting your dress next weekend?" Molly asked.

"My dress?"

"For the Mid-March dance."

I looked over at Raz. "You didn't tell me I needed a fancy dress."

"Not a formal, like a Sunday dress," Molly said. "I'm wearing the one from last year."

She described it in detail, from its high low hem to the flounces of ruffles that fell from the waist on down.

"My mom got me a new shrug this year because you know the rules." Molly rolled her eyes. "If it has spaghetti straps it has to be covered. Last year's was fuzzy. The one she's bringing this year is all sequins."

I so wanted access to a computer so I could start looking at dresses online. Mom would be in heaven going from store to store, and Dad would drag along because he had to. But all our time together would involve me and dressing rooms. Unless...

During study time I wrote to my folks and asked if they could bring three of the dresses in my closet. Nobody here had seen any of my dress-up stuff. My dad would be thrilled if I saved him money for once, and Mom would be happy enough buying me shoes and jewelry. Maybe we could see a movie, too, if we shopped fast.

With that checked off my list of things to worry about, I was in a great mood for the rest of the night. I actually finished all my homework during study time, even my sketch of a formal dining room for home décor class. I finally figured out how to use the sheets of graph paper, although it would be tons easier to use a computer. But no, only seniors got to do computer design. We underclass peons had to use paper and pencil. Not that I was bitter or anything.

At bed check time, I was under the covers pretending to be asleep. As soon as the hallway was quiet, I got up, turned on my light and practiced the magic Morry had taught me so far. The spelling bee was at the end of May. It was almost the first of March. I'd better practice a lot more than I had so far.

****

By the February parents' weekend, Snick had me ordering parts and taking inventory. He and Mr. Morrison had made an arrangement. I'd learn the mechanics at school and the business part from Snick. He promised me that as soon as he got a chain saw to fix he'd let me help. He also said that if I stuck around until spring, he'd teach me the basics of electricity and plumbing too. I figured the worst I could do was shock us both until our teeth rattled or flood the entire town, so I said sure, I wanted to do that.

150

Miss Willowood made a huge production of the weekend again. Fancy food, big cake and that fake smile as she greeted the moms. The dads, of course, got the real thing and lots of attention. Most of them, like my father, were polite but fast to find their kids. This time I had so much to tell them. My mom seemed happy, and when we went up with Wendy to get cake, I heard her whisper to my dad, "Violet seems to have finally settled in."

Shopping was so much fun this time because we had a purpose besides making my parents feel less guilty for sending me here. Mom even tried on shoes, too. I laughed until I fell over watching her try to walk in five-inch stilettos. For the first time since Dad brought me here, they were treating me like they used to. You know, like an ordinary kid.

I so wanted to tell them about Raz asking me to the dance and my going to be in the spelling bee. But I didn't want to spoil our time together with a lecture on following the rules.

The weekend whizzed by and before I was ready, Mom had straightened up my always neat room and made me try on all three dresses with my new shoes and jewelry. For a minute I thought she was going to cry. Mom cries every time something happens in my life. Sometimes it's a happy cry and sometimes it's a life totally sucks cry, but her supply of tears is endless. Dad started his "Love you, honey, but we've got to go" routine which meant he thought she was going to bawl, too. I didn't blame him for hustling her out. I wouldn't want to listen to my mom's sobbing for three hours either.

Worn out but happy, I went down the hall to Wendy's room. Molly and Muffy were in there, so I guess their folks were gone too. I made them all come back and look at my dresses. Wendy liked the one my mom picked, the red one with the full skirt. Molly liked the yellow one, and Muffy thought the hot pink dress was the best of the three. Okay, so they weren't that much help, but it was fun anyway. And I liked doing something girly after all the time I'd been spending with greasy parts and planting soil.

I filled two whole pages in my journal that night. When I was old and sitting around remembering my life, I wanted to be able to read them again and remember what the last couple of weeks were like. I hardly ever thought about Green Hills and the friends I left behind anymore. And although I had to put up with Miss Willowood, it wasn't as bad as reporting to Mr. Winters' office. At least I had Miss Tiddums and Mr. Morrison here.

****

Our seeds sprouted super-fast or at least it seemed like it. I explained that I have a black thumb and all plants die under my care, but they made me transplant the seedlings any way. We didn't have to put our names on them or anything, but I knew the teacher would know which ones were mine. The dead ones.

I got back my outline on the stupid book with a couple of suggestions. My dining room design got an A, and it looked like my mid-term grades would be okay. Not college prep at Green Hills good, but then again, not rough enough to put my parents in shock.

I was blazing good at my out-of-school lessons though. Morry said I had magic fingers, and Miss Tiddums baked so many cupcakes and muffins to celebrate that I was afraid I wouldn't be able to fit in any of the dresses my folks had brought. Since none of us thought Miss Willowood would be willing to send in an application from Hempstead, Miss Tiddums had taken care of it.

"Violet, dear," she said, "she only has a bachelor's degree and specialized classes. I have two master's degrees and a PhD. There will be no problem."

Even though I thought that sounded sketchy, she was right. Turned out the guidance counselor didn't have to submit the application as long as two other members of the staff would sign on the dotted line. Morry and Miss Tiddums took care of that.

I was dying to know what spells would be required this year. Miss Tiddums said they sent that information out super close to the spelling bee so nobody would concentrate just on the required magic. So Morry taught me a whole bunch of different stuff that he thought would get me through a couple of rounds at least.

****

I was mucho surprised by my appointment to the dance committee. Ollie was on it, but the others were kids I didn't know very well. They all knew me, the new girl. I was thinking "awkward" as I walked into the art room where the planning meeting was, but they all treated me nice. I sat and listened since I didn't even know there was a dance until a couple of weeks ago. I nodded when everyone else decided on a clovers and leprechaun theme because of St. Patrick's Day. I kinda lost track trying to figure which dress of mine went best with green. Yellow was so overdone, and blue would be stupid. The choice was easy. Hot pink. I had to remember to tell Raz.

Thinking about Raz made me wish that I could tell him what I was really doing when I went to Snick's shop. I mean, what I was doing besides the fixing stuff part. I bet he'd think it was cool that I was going to represent the academy. But if I told him, I'd break my promise to Morry and Miss Tiddums. And not that he'd do it on purpose, but Raz might tell another of the Terribles, and then they'd all know.

Having the dance on a Saturday made it all that much better. Our committee had Friday evening to decorate the ballroom, and then we girls could use Saturday to get beautiful. Two of the trusted senior girls were allowed to go to town and pick out everything we'd need, so we spent a lot of time making a list for them.

My happy almost went away the Monday before the dance. It was a huge day in our engines class. After all our time rebuilding our lawnmower engines, Mr. Morrison was going to let us fire them

155

up. The guys tried to pretend it was no big deal, but I was practically vibrating from excitement. Working with Snick had boosted my confidence. I was sure mine would come to life on the first try and purr like a kitten until I shut it off.

Mr. Morrison is nobody's fool. He made us all stand back, and then, one at a time, we got to go up and start the mowers. Greg was first, and he took a bow when it ran perfectly. A couple other guys started theirs up, too, and then it was time for Raz to perform.

He winked at me as he stepped up to his workbench. He pushed the choke button a couple of times and then pulled on the rope. His lawn mower roared to life.

And burst into flames ten seconds later.

Mr. Morrison went running for the fire extinguisher shouting "Safety glasses on! Get into the classroom!" as he went. We poured into the adjacent room and watched through the glass window at Raz backed into a corner and the fire extinguisher pouring a steam of white stuff over the motor. Mr. Morrison sprayed from side to side and all around the mower until the foam covered everything. He motioned for Raz to come out of his hiding place.

Raz being Raz, he stepped right into that chemical stuff, and his foot slid out from under him. He grabbed for whatever he could find to stop his fall, which turned out to be Mr. Morrison. The two of them hung onto each other's shoulders, the red fire extinguisher between them, and slipped and slid their way to safety.

The guys around me were all cracking up. I tried hard not to laugh because I was afraid Raz might see me and get mad. Or Mr. Morrison might see me and sentence me to cleaning up the mess. But I couldn't help myself when they started going around in circles as if they were dancing, which made the guys bust up.

Poor Raz. His clothes and boots were covered with white clumps, his safety glasses were covered with the stuff, but his face was bright red from what I was sure was embarrassment and not heat from the fire. I so wanted to rush out there and help him, but I was still trying to be one of the guys. They'd rag on him, not wipe him off with shop rags.

Mr. Morrison came into the classroom and told us to sit down and work on our engine diagrams. He put Greg in charge, which was like letting the monkeys run the zoo. They all goofed off until Mr.

157

Morrison came back to tell us Raz had been checked out by the school nurse and he was fine except that he had to take shower and change clothes.

At dinner I waited for him to say something about it. He didn't. So I didn't either. It wasn't because he's the closest thing I've had to a boyfriend since I got here but because I didn't want him to feel any worse about it. So he's a klutz. I think that makes him interesting.

He sat down next to me during study time with this weird look on his face. He leaned real close and whispered, "If you don't want to go to the dance with me anymore, it's okay."

I stared at him, trying to figure out what he meant. Was he backing out? Or did he think that what happened in engine class would make me not like him anymore?

"If you don't want to go with me, just say so." I sounded a whole lot more ticked off than I was.

"No." Raz looked stricken. "That's not what I meant."

I smiled to try to make him feel better. "Too late to back out now," I said. "I've already decided on my dress."

"Is it shamrock green?" he teased.

"You'll have to wait and see."

That was the last thing either of us said because the art teacher was in charge tonight. She pointed at us and put a finger to her lips. I started working on my stupid book report again and tried to pretend Raz wasn't sitting right next to me worried about whether I still liked him.

Chapter Ten

The ballroom looked, well, less ballroomish.
Maybe the wallpaper and big columns were in style
when they built this place, but before we decorated, it
reminded me of my parents' country club. All it
needed was a bunch of old people sitting around
talking about golf.

Now it looked almost cool. I figured we'd
have streamers and cardboard cutouts, but the senior
girls came through in a big way. A runner of green
carpet covered the marble floor where everyone
would come in, and black plastic pots full of those
gold candy coins sat in the middle of each table.
Green ferns along the walls hid a lot of the hideous
wallpaper.

The fake rocks were the best part. I knew they
were just plastic, but they looked real. We moved
them around until we made a kind of cave that people

could stand in to have their picture taken. Describing it is hard, but the ballroom really was sweet by the time we were done.

I practiced my illusions in my room that night even though I really didn't feel like it. The closer we got to the spelling bee, the more I wondered why I ever agreed to do this. Kids were going to be using real magic. They didn't need sneakiness and fast hands to get by.

Morry was great when I found the guts to tell him. He sat down on one of the stools in Snick's shop, looked me right in the eye and said, "Violet, you're doing nothing wrong. You're not cheating. I read the rules thoroughly before I sent in your application. Nowhere does it say natural magic is required."

Knowing I wasn't breaking the rules made me feel better. At least about the spelling bee. I did have a little twinge of feeling bad about my dance date but not enough to break Raz's heart.

****

Saturday was a perfect day. Even though it was a little chilly, the sun came through the ballroom windows to illuminate the decorations. I heard the rumor at breakfast that the food for the dance was

161

coming from a caterer instead of our kitchen. And I heard that Miss Willowood had gone to the dentist because she had an infected tooth.

Unless she came to the dance stoned, no way was she going to be there to chaperone. I didn't care who took her place. The whole night would be better without her yelling at anyone she thought was dancing too close.

The day dragged by. I was so nervous I could hardly eat lunch, and I despaired of my hair looking like anything but a straggly mess. Muffy came to my room with her straightener and hair spray and managed to turn it into something. We rummaged through my drawer of hair stuff until we found a gold and fake diamond hair clip that was perfect.

I returned the favor by helping Muffy with her makeup. I knew she liked one of the senior boys. Making her as beautiful as possible might get him to dance with her, which would be beyond awesome. I gave her sexy model eyes by copying a magazine picture and made her cheekbones higher with some of my own peach blush.

We were, I decided as we stood together in front of my mirror at six o'clock, gorgeous beyond compare. Giggling, we linked arms and skipped

162

down the hall to the stairs. Peeking over the railing, we saw a bunch of other kids there already. Raz was with them, looking toward the stairs for me.

"Ready?" Muffy asked.

"Ready." I nodded for her to go down first. I intended to make an entrance, thank you.

Since we weren't supposed to be together, I just said hi when I walked past Raz—which I did slowly so he could get the full effect of my beauty. The art teacher stood behind a table near the ballroom entrance and called a few of us over as we went by. I was so surprised when she called my name and then handed me a white box. I thanked her and pulled out the card that tucked into it. I turned to see Raz smiling big at me.

I laughed when I read the card: "Surprise, grease monkey!"

The wrist corsage inside the box had green and white carnations with a hot pink ribbon. I figure one of the girl Terribles had tipped him off about my dress so he could get the corsage to match. I slid the elastic band over my hand and adjusted the flowers. I wondered how many of the other girls with flowers had gotten them from their secret dates.

Turned out that the rumors were right. The dinner before the dance was so not standard academy fare. The roast pork loin was delicious, the baby red potatoes fell apart and the spears of asparagus had the same hollandaise sauce like my mom makes. When a caterer in a black uniform wheeled a dessert cart around to every table, I thought it was the most elegant thing I'd ever seen. Trust me, choosing between cheesecake with cherry topping and the most delicious-looking chocolate cake I'd ever seen was not easy.

Even though we could sit with anybody we wanted, the Terribles all ended up at the same table. Naturally. It wouldn't have been the same if we hadn't all been together. Everybody looked so different in their fancy clothes, though. The guys had on suits and every girl had gotten as dressed up as she could.

If this was some sort of fairy tale teen movie, there would have been a real orchestra in the ballroom and Raz and I would have danced all night under one of those old disco balls. But this was Hempstead Academy. The music teacher doubled as the deejay. She was slow, but she tried hard and even wore a ball cap on sideways. We decided she got points for trying.

No surprise, the guys went to the tables on one side and the girls went to the other side. A couple of guys asked some girl to dance on the first song but most of the boys waited until the second one to come over and ask us. Raz said, "Wanna dance?" as if the thought had never occurred to him until now. I shrugged and said sure.

For a clumsy guy, he danced well. We made sure not to break the rules and kept space between us. Even so it felt good to have his arms around me. He smiled at me as we danced, but he didn't say anything. It was like he didn't want to spoil the moment. Which was fine with me. Just being with him like this was good.

The music changed into a song with a hard beat. Raz and I stayed out on the floor because there were no superstar dancers out there, so we fit right in. When Raz caught his foot sideways on the marble and almost fell over, I started laughing so hard I actually snorted. The music was loud enough for him not to hear, thank goodness. We gave up though and went to a table to sit down.

So we just happened to be sitting there when the double doors swung open and in walked Miss Willowood in all her glory, fancy dress and all. One side of her face was puffy, and she moved like the drunk old ladies at the country club, stumbling a little as she walked. Her words were slurred as she yelled "No nasty moves!" at the dancers so I think she was lost in a pain-drug-induced haze. Too bad she had that duty-first thing going on. The dance would have been a lot better if she'd just gone to bed and forgotten all about us.

The other teachers tried to make her leave. If she'd been fifty pounds thinner or the soccer coach fifty pounds bigger, she would have hauled her out of there without help. She tried. Miss Willowood resisted. So they kinda staggered around for a while and almost knocked over the plastic rock cave. That made a bunch of kids run over for a block the coach should have loved. That didn't work either.

Mr. Morrison jumped into the battle. With him on one side and the coach on the other, a drooling and protesting Miss Willowood left the room in a style none of us would ever forget. Even the temporary deejay stopped spinning discs to watch the commotion.

Best of all, the photographer hired to take our photos in the cave captured the departure with Miss Willowood's best side showing—her rear end. He could make a fortune selling copies around the academy.

Once the fuss subsided the music started up again and the dance floor kinda filled. Raz's confidence was up so we headed back out there again. Ollie was dancing with Muffy, and they both looked like they were having fun. Molly and Wendy weren't dancing, but they were at a table talking to a couple of boys, their heads bouncing and their arms flying as they talked.

A few songs later we joined them, hot and thirsty from dancing. A cheer went up when the doors opened again and two carts rolled in One held a big punch bowl and cups and the other one had little containers of ice cream on the top shelf and cupcakes on the lower one. The boys told us to sit there and they'd bring our refreshments to us. Wendy pretended to swoon from shock, and we all laughed harder than we should have.

The night ended way too soon. I danced as much as I could with Raz without raising suspicions. We both danced with enough others to make it look like we were with the program, but we found each other for the last dance.

To make sure we all behaved, the girls left the dance in one big group. The boys had to wait until we were all upstairs before they could leave. I so wanted a goodbye kiss from Raz or even a hug but had to settle for a wave in his direction.

My feet were still floating when I shouted goodnight to Wendy and the other girls in my wing. I hated to take off my dress and make-up because I was afraid the magic would slip away when I became just plain old Violet again. I was wrong. I still felt all bubbly inside as I settled down under my blankets with Alfredo who seemed really interested in all the details of the dance.

"I like Raz," I whispered to my silent confidante. "Really, really like him."

****

Sunday was a quiet day. After chapel and lunch, I forced myself to work on the stupid book report. My theory was the sooner I got it done, the happier I'd be. But the good feeling from yesterday was still there, so even writing about the traveling losers didn't seem as awful as it should have. I rewarded myself by re-reading a book I loved and couldn't believe it when the announcement for dinner came.

Raz reached the table before me. He got a great big grin on his face when he saw me. I bet he wanted to kiss me as much as I wanted him to.

"You look happy," he said when I sat down next to him.

"Yeah, because I almost finished that book report."

Raz laughed. "That the only reason?"

"Maybe there's one more," I said.

"Good." He turned around to high-five Ollie when he slid into the chair next to him. Before long we were all there. We started talking about, duh, the dance until Ollie put his hands over his ears and said, "No more. No…more!"

That started us laughing. We were in a great mood when our table's turn came and we went to get our food. That mood lasted all through the meal, which was a hideous combination of ziti pasta in watery sauce, canned pears and corn with red peppers in it. Trust me, all through it I kept thinking of Miss Tiddums' cooking.

Sunday is a TV night. The shows they let us watch are only a step above PG, but at least that's better than little kid cartoons. Raz and I sat in the middle of the Terribles, and he took my hand for a little while. I guess he figured it was safe with our friends all around us, but all I could see in my mind was Miss Willowood walking in and catching us. He dropped my hand when they passed out popcorn and didn't take it again. I wish he had despite the threat of Miss Willowood hanging over us.

Monday was back to class and back to my magic lessons. Morry had the date for the spelling bee: May 21. Seeing my name on the approved list made me realize this was really going to happen. I was going to the spelling bee, and I'd be competing against my old school.

Which made me think about Mr. Winters and hope my mom took a camera because I wanted a picture of his face when I got up on that stage. The last time I saw the man was in his office talking about how I needed to be in a special place for people like me. And we were about to meet again.

I finally voiced my fear.

"What if I lose in the first round?" I hoped I didn't sound like a pathetic whiner. "I don't want to slink back here in shame."

Morry chuckled. "You won't lose in the first round. You're already good enough to make it into the semi-finals."

"But what if I do?"

"Then you'll be the first one out instead of someone from Mongrove High or Stewart Prep."

Okay, he was right. Someone had to be first loser. So I'd work extra hard and make sure it wasn't me. I leaned against the counter in Snick's workroom and tried to figure how Morry made an egg disappear and then appear again.

****

"Miss Greene, please stay after class." Miss Willowood's out-of-breath voice echoed slightly in the engine shop. As soon as she waddled back out, the smart-ass comments started. I pretended they were being super funny with "Been nice knowing you, Violet" and "Oh-oh, you're in trouble." I was too nervous to fire back at them. I knew, just knew, she'd found out about my secret date with Raz.

Except she didn't tell him to stay behind. My nervousness deepened into dread. I was going back to battling office machines. I just knew it.

I fumbled trying to put the spark plug in the engine and almost knocked everything off my bench

171

as I grabbed for the plug before it could go rolling under the lockers. Greg and Raz both jumped up and helped me keep the engine parts from erupting into the nearby workspaces. Mr. Morrison left the kid he was helping and came over to make sure everything was all right.

"What does she want?" I muttered low enough that nobody could hear but him.

"No clue." Mr. Morrison looked right into my eyes. "Don't worry. You're stronger than her."

That made me feel so much better. He was right. His little smile made me realize he had enjoyed Miss Willowood's humiliation at the dance too.

I'd just gotten everything put away when the announcement came to change classes. As everybody else walked out talking, I went into the classroom with Mr. Morrison. I had just slid into my chair when Miss Willowood walked in, her eyes boring into me. Mr. Morrison's
"You're stronger than her" echoed in my head. I met her stare and offered a smile.

She so didn't expect that. I was supposed to be cowering in my seat, scared of what was going to happen next. I figured she couldn't take too long since I still had one more class to go. What kind of a guidance counselor made yelling at a student more important than educating one?

Not Miss Willowood.

"Miss Greene."

I answered with the expected "Yes, ma'am?"

"I believe your need for special tutoring has been satisfied. I will expect you to spend your time immediately after classes developing your social skills rather than going to that disreputable repair place." Her face looked like she was sucking on a lemon. Her lips were tight and her eyes were narrow slits. "All students are given equal treatment. I do hope you understand that no one child can expect to be specialer than the others."

Specialer? I managed to keep my mouth shut for once and not tell her she meant "more special." I did notice, though, that Mr. Morrison had his hand over his mouth like he was concentrating. Or trying to shove back a laugh.

"Yes, ma'am," I said again.

"Then you are dismissed." Miss Willowood turned on her heel and marched out. The door had barely closed behind her before Mr. Morrison exploded. I started laughing too and was five minutes late to class because it took me so long to quit. Good guy that he is, Mr. Morrison wrote me an excuse that said nothing about the high and mighty guidance counselor of Hempstead Academy.

****

"How did this happen, Lydia?" Al wished he could reach through the phone line and choke the woman.

"I knew nothing about it. Nothing at all."

"I didn't ask what you knew. I asked how this happened."

He listened impatiently to the woman's excuses. Any shred of respect he'd had for her was gone. Lydia Willowood had lost control of her students. Plain and simple, she should lose her job for this. Unfortunately that wasn't his decision. The elusive principal of Hempstead Academy was the only who could do that. And that was an impossibility considering that the man was on a six-month leave of absence to study methods of teaching in Argentina.

"Who signed the application?" He interrupted the steady flow of words.

"Our school psychologist and a member of our teaching staff."

"That's highly irregular."

Lydia's voice was sharp as she retorted, "I was under the influence of medication after oral surgery. I certainly can't be blamed for allowing trusted faculty members to pick up the slack."

Oh, there were so many things Al wanted to say to her. He held his tongue. He had no choice but to keep the woman as a partner until this dreadful situation was resolved. Surely she could study the school's student handbook and find some loophole. Any administrator worth his salt knew there were always loopholes.

Of course, she was only a counselor trusted to advise children and not to protect the school's purpose and reputation. He knew the pair who actually signed the application. After all, one of them was the school psychologist. This whole farce might simply be an exercise in boosting the Greene girl's self-confidence. Nevertheless, he refused to allow as prestigious a competition as the spelling bee to be corrupted.

"Five weeks," he said. "That's how much time you have between the time I hang up and the competition begins. I trust you will ensure that Violet Greene will not be participating."

175

"I didn't know you could withdraw a competitor."

"Only if they're gravely ill and she never missed a day of school." Al's voice was grim. "So find some other way to do it. No matter what it takes."

Chapter Eleven

I lay on my bed staring up at the ceiling. Facts
were undeniable. That's what my science teachers
always said. And the fact was that in twenty-seven
days I'd be on a stage trying to fake my way toward a
title that any student in the district would kill to win.
Figuratively. It was more like any student except us
academy types would turn their fiercest foe into a
razor back hog or maybe a fat tomato.

Morry kept me after class under the pretense
of talking about degunking a choke. What he did
instead was spring a big one on me. He wanted me to
have one huge trick up my sleeve. That trick, he
decided, would be levitation.

Levitation!

I sighed and flopped over to stare at the wall.
I'd learned a lot so far. I might be able to pull off
making pencils dance across the table and making
torn playing cards whole again. Levitation meant

something would float like a balloon with no contact to any surface. I might be able to make a flowerpot or something go up in the air, but Morry had decided I was going to levitate. Me, whose feet had never left the ground. And who was very happy that way.

"I'm afraid." I confessed my secret to Alfredo. "If the judges think my magic is real, I have to leave here. And if they don't, maybe they'll kick me out of here for cheating." Tears threatened to spill. "I don't want to spend the rest of my life washing dishes. Or marrying somebody who digs ditches. Oh, Alfredo, I never should have said yes!"

That's when I started crying for real. It wasn't really about the spelling bee though. It was about everything. Not being able to say goodbye to everyone before I was dragged here. Living away from my parents, which sucked. Missing my place on the academic team and struggling to learn all that stuff about flowers and bushes.

And how totally disgusting my life would be without Raz and the rest of the Terribles. Especially Raz.

Alfredo lay curled against my chest and listened. One thing about him was that he's a great listener. I'd been telling him my secrets like forever, and he'd never let a single one of them slip. I wondered if anyone would ever understand why a stuffed bear is my very best friend in the whole world.

****

"A bunch of us are going outside and play soccer." Raz slammed his books down on the seat beside me and turned toward me.

"I can't. I have to study."

He sighed. "It seems like you always have to study."

Oh, that was a knife jabbed into my heart. I wanted to spend every minute I could with Raz, but the spelling bee was only twenty-one days away. I actually had faith that rounds one and two were doable. Morry's confidence that I could go all the way up to the semi-finals or maybe even the finals was driving me crazy. I was practicing as hard as I could. I almost asked my folks if they could only come on the Sunday of parents' weekend because I was worried about passing my finals. I hated to lie to them. I hated to lie to anyone. But every minute I didn't work on it was one moment that kept me from floating cross-legged from the yoga mat where I practiced.

179

"You don't understand," I protested. "I transferred mid-year and then I changed classes. My dad will kill me if my grades drop from what they were at Green Hills."

"I do understand. Honest." Raz took both my hands in his and stared into my eyes. "I like you, Violet. Really like you."

"Me too. Really like you, I mean."

He grinned. "So we're cool. I'll play. You work. As long as you're thinking about me."

Raz grabbed his books and left with a wave. I was so tempted to play hooky from practicing, but I could almost sense Morry behind me telling me we only had three more weeks until I stepped on that stage. Three weeks which also included a landscape plan in horticulture and the very last, I hoped, rewrite of my report on *The Grapes of Wrath*. I deserved a gold medal for all the times I'd read the name Joad.

The study room was almost empty since it was still that free time the academy kept telling our parents was wonderful for us. I sat at a desk as far away from the two girls on the other side of the room and took out my pad of graph paper. Once again I realized how hard it was back in the old days before people had computers, tablets and smart phones.

With the laptop I had to leave at home, I could have found a program, knocked out the garden plan and been done in five minutes. I tried not to think about that as I pulled a ruler and pencil from my backpack. No matter what my parents thought, old school was not cool.

The announcement for dinner made me jump in my seat. I'd been so into my homework that I'd lost track of time. I jammed everything in my pack and hurried upstairs to stick it in my room. The last thing I expected to see was a pink box with a ribbon sitting next to my door.

If I'd been a cat, I would have been dead from curiosity before I got the door open and my backpack tossed inside. I glanced up and down the hall but didn't see boxes by any other door. Of course maybe we all got one and I was just the last person to come to my room.

I put the box on the bed and took off the lid. I laughed when I saw what was inside. I didn't need the note I found to realize Miss Tiddums had dropped by and left me a stack of smiley-face cookies. A glance at the clock on my desk reminded me I didn't have time to try one. I had exactly four minutes to get into my chair at the table.

181

Another thirty seconds and I'd have made it. I dropped into my seat. Miss Willowood, tonight's monitor, glared at me. I knew I was in trouble when she pushed back from the table and headed in my direction. Luck intervened. Before she could reach our table, Mr. Morrison intercepted her. I was too far away to hear what he said but he winked in my direction as he escorted her to the dessert table. Breathing a quiet word of thanks, I started asking Raz about the soccer game.

I kinda missed some details because I kept thinking about how he said he liked me, really liked me. I had to tell him about what Morry and I were doing or I'd bust. But I'd promised not to tell anybody, and I was so not the person who went back on her word.

Tell him or don't tell him. That's all I could think about when he took the chair across from me during study time. The one thing I didn't want was for Raz to hate me when he learned the truth and wonder why I hadn't trusted him enough to share the plan.

The final draft of my book report and the landscape design were both finished before study time was over. If I hadn't been sitting by Raz, I would have asked permission to go to my room early. Every moment of practice time counted now. But so did being with Raz. When the spelling bee was over, Raz would still be around. And I knew he wouldn't care if I won or lost, only that I tried to make the academy part of the real school world.

As the final seconds of study time ticked down, Raz shoved a note to me. I didn't have time to read it before the announcement came to return to our rooms which is what he'd planned, I guessed. I stuck the note inside my binder and joined Wendy for the walk up to our wing. She was all excited about the end of the semester coming because she was going home for the summer.

"Last year I stayed here for summer session."

"Summer session?" Green Hills never had summer classes. I didn't know any school ever did.

Wendy's usually happy face was solemn. "There were six of us. That's all. Six sets of parents who didn't want their kids."

I wanted to say something to make her feel better, but I didn't know what. One thing I've always known is that my parents love me and like having me around. Wendy had pictures of her mom and dad in her room and they looked okay. Maybe I was missing something. Like her mom had some horrible disease they were keeping Wendy from knowing about and her dad's entire life was taken up with caring for her mother. Yeah, I knew that probably wasn't true, but I couldn't imagine any other reason for not caring.

I know Wendy loves her folks, even if the situation is sketchy, or she wouldn't look so sad. I so wanted to tell her about the spelling bee because that would cheer her up. Nobody roots for the underdog quite like Wendy. But I'd promised. And besides, Raz would probably think I didn't trust him if I told her and not him.

Whoa, this whole thing was getting complicated. All that blah, blah, blah of my dad's about how lying is its own punishment was beginning to make sense. I couldn't confess that to him, though. He'd start telling me all sorts of other stuff meant to make me the perfect person on earth, and I could only take so much of that.

"You want to come to my room and celebrate that you're going home?" I said on an impulse. I still had some chocolate candy left over from when my mom and dad came the last time. Between the two of us, we could polish it off and not feel too guilty about how much we ate.

"Can't." Wendy sighed as she shook her head. "I have to draw a map of Europe by Friday for my world government class and I haven't even started. Maybe we can do it later, okay?"

"Sure." I waved goodbye as she reached her door and I kept on walking. She was like the coolest person I knew. Except Raz. And maybe the other Terribles. They were all super cool, the best friends I'd ever had.

Alone behind the closed door of my room, I pulled out the note and grinned. "All work and no play makes Violet a tired girl," Raz had written. He'd drawn a goofy cartoon of me all bent over with a bunch of books on my back. Somehow he always knew how to make me feel better.

*****

Mr. Morrison had begun calling me the "mechanical mastermind" since I figured out a way to hook an engine to a red wagon and make it self-propelled—on paper anyway. The engine was sitting in the shop, but I didn't have a wagon, and the academy wasn't going to let me experiment anyway. Independent thought was not highly appreciated at good old Hempstead.

185

Neither would my embarrassing the entire school. So I dropped my books on my desk and started practicing my illusions harder than I ever had. I was so nervous about the floating thing that I fumbled the rope trick which was like the first one I'd ever learned. I threw myself across the bed and started taking deep breaths. My mother was all into yoga and meditation, and that's what she did when life made her crazy. She must have done it differently, though, because before long my lungs ached. So I did what any sensible person would do.

I took a shower. A long shower.

The steady spray of water gave me lots of alone time to visualize myself on that stage beating every other person Until the final rounds anyway. Every time I tried to see myself floating in the air, I saw myself falling down, down, down instead. Morry may have had complete confidence in me, but he wasn't going to be out there, was he?

The water was getting cold before I got out. I had made a decision. Unless I was super good in one week exactly, levitation was a no-go. I also decided to wait those full seven days before I told Morry. Actually, I was hoping that at the end of seven days of failure he'd catch a clue and change things up.

This time my practice was so smooth that I almost believed I had a ton of natural magic as I watched myself in the mirror. Quick hands, easy movements and total confidence. That's what Morry said I needed.

I found out the next day that there was more.

"What do you mean there's questions on the theories of natural magic?" Panic made me forget I was talking to a teacher and an elder to boot. But Morry ignored my rudeness.

"A five question interview with a three-scholar panel," he read from the instructions for sponsoring teachers. He looked straight at me. "You're smart, Violet. This should be a snap for you."

"But what if I have to do something?" I curled my arms around myself "What if they make me demonstrate what I'm talking about?"

"Then you will demonstrate it." Miss Tiddums, who was sitting on the other end of the couch from Morry, said in the sternest tone I'd ever heard her use. "I refuse to allow you to underestimate your abilities. What the others take for granted, you've had to work at. As far as I'm concerned, you're going in with a huge advantage."

I buried my face in my hands. Yeah, I'd taken the required study of elemental magic when I was a freshman, but that was two years ago. I'd forgotten everything I'd learned except that essentially magic is the harnessing of the human mind in a positive way. If, of course, you had at least a tiny bit of magic in your genes.

I remember, too, that the teacher had explained that because of recessive genes lining up just right, a few unlucky souls were born without magic. I'd kinda tuned that part out. Now I wish I hadn't since I was one of them now.

"Violet." Miss Tiddums called my name in a softer but still no-nonsense voice. I peeked through my fingers at her.

"You're not being thrown to the wolves. I'll leave study material for you in Mr. Morrison's class. Take it home and start reading. If it turns out that you're truly not suited for this, then you won't do it. I can sign an affidavit that you're not in the right mental state to compete."

"I'm sure that won't bother Al Winters a bit."

Mr. Winters. My basset hound-faced nemesis. The man who'd made my mother cry in public.

"And Miss Willowood will surely be delighted as well."

I threw up my arms. "Okay, I get it. Success is the best revenge, or whatever that saying is. I'll dazzle the judges and wow the audience with my poise and finesse."

Morry laughed. Miss Tiddums grinned and announced she believed there was a warm blueberry pie in the kitchen. I was again so grateful she'd convinced the board that as a transfer student so late in the year, I needed deeper counseling than Miss Willowood could provide. I kinda felt guilty but not too much. She was counseling me. So was Mr. Morrison. I just hoped no one asked what that counseling was about.

****

"Once again, Violet." I groaned and thumped my head against the table. Maybe if I jiggled my brain I could remember all this stupid stuff. "What are the three attributes of fire?"

I raised my head and took a deep breath.

"Brightness, motion and...thinness!"

"Excellent!" Morry settled himself on top of his teacher's desk. "Now for an easier one. What are the four basic elements?"

189

"I gots this!" I stood up and did a little dance because this one was easy. "Earth, fire, wind and water."

Two thumbs up from Morry and another question.

"What are the conditions of the second order of natural magic?"

Whoa. We moved into areas that my brain seriously didn't want to recognize. I ran through what I'd learned in my head. According to Plato, some dude from ancient times, the elements were three-fold. Four elements, three characteristics of each. Which were …

"Compounded, changeable and impure!" I shouted.

"And she wins again!" Morry shouted back. We both started to laugh not because anything was particularly funny but because I might, just might, know enough to fool the judges. When we both finally settled down, Morry fired another question at me.

"For the million dollar prize, what are the immutables?"

"Time, space and substance?"

"You are absolutely right." Morry held his hand out for a fist bump. "Now please demonstrate pryomancy for this panel."

Pyro. That was fire. Every element had a mancy, which was the old-fashioned name for magical stuff. I nodded and stretched out my hands to show them to him. Then I brought my fingertips to my forehead as if I was concentrating, brought my hands back down and rubbed them together. Within seconds flames danced on my palm.

"Most impressive," Miss Tiddums said from where she'd been watching. "If I didn't know better, I'd say that was as natural as it comes."

I was so happy when she brought out lemonade and fat sugar-topped cookies. That meant this session was over. The spelling bee was only a couple weeks away and the end of school three weeks after that. I could not believe it was almost time for summer break. It seemed like I'd just walked into this place like last week.

Mr. Morrison had requested that I be his student assistant. Miss Willowood hadn't been too happy, but when he explained that the boys horsed around and never cleaned up she had to say yes. Not that she worried me. I had Miss Tiddums on my side, after all, which was kinda like traveling through the world with a lion. Or a ferocious grizzly bear.

Miss Tiddums handed me a folder and told me to read it that night.

"The originals are quite old and can't be taken from the research section at the university library," she said. "But the scanner on my phone works quite well. I thought you might find a tidbit or two in there that could be helpful."

I hugged her, even though I know students aren't supposed to hug teachers and vice versa. But I couldn't think of her as a teacher during these times. She was my friend, my very good friend.

****

"I'm normally a patient man, Lydia, but when I reach the end of my rope, it's not pretty."

Lydia Willowood's hand tightened on the phone. Al Winters seemed irritated. At her. She sensed trouble ahead.

"Perhaps this sort of thing is easy at your school, but we respect the rights of our students here," she retorted.

"One student." Al said the words slowly. "I have asked you to keep an eye on one student, a mousy little girl who appreciates authority. Why is this so difficult for you?"

Lydia wished her hand were on Al's throat. She'd show him difficult. As in impossible to breathe because she was squeezing the life out of him. How dare this man speak to her like that. She had a very prestigious bachelor's degree and spent nearly all last summer in enhanced training on working with difficult adolescents. She'd never gotten anything less than a perfect job evaluation, and everyone knew the students loved her. That much was obvious by the way they smiled when she came near. All heads turned toward her for a reason after all.

"I am not in the habit of spying." She struggled to keep her tone cordial. "Besides I believe if there is fault, it lies with you. Neither of us would have to deal with this if you tracked your students better."

"Now listen." Anger was evident in Al's voice. "She never made a minimum magic score at Green Hills. Our goal is to bring out the best in every student. Our hope was that she was simply nervous and did poorly on tests."

"Oh, hogwash." Lydia was over it now. "Her grades were excellent which made up for some of

193

your magically-talented kids who couldn't count to twenty without using their toes. Magic is important on how schools rate, yes, but plain old-fashioned learning is too. Now instead of blaming each other, we need to find a way to keep her away from the competition."

"I'd think you'd want her there if that's the case," Al huffed. "Or don't you people care if your students have potential?"

Enough was enough. Lydia felt her face flush and her heart start to race.

"And be called before the board because you screwed up? We have high standards, and our children don't have to rely on trickery to get through life."

"Trickery?" Al bellowed. "Say that again and I'll have you up on charges before the district committee on magical arts!"

"And they will tell you our specialty is working with children who start life with a strike against them. Yours is, what, to make sure you get promoted to grand poo-bah?"

The silence greeting her remark grew to an uncomfortable length. She fidgeted in her desk chair. Maybe she'd gone too far and he would have her brought up on charges. Her mouth had always said that her attitude would get her in trouble someday and this might be the day.

"I think we both need to calm down," Al said in a strangled voice. "And it might be better if we discussed this in person. Say, over lunch tomorrow? In a neutral location?"

When he suggested the Vernon Café at noon, she agreed. It was halfway between the schools and a place where she doubted they'd see anyone they knew. Although she wouldn't mind if they were seen. Word might get back, and a certain small engine and automotive instructor could hear. Men were so easy to decipher. They always wanted what someone else had. And while Al Winters was a good catch, he wasn't the only fish in the sea. Or the nearest one.

Chapter Twelve

Al hadn't been to the Vernon for quite a long time, but the place hadn't changed. It still had white curtains, fake greenery in fancy pots and, best of all, high-backed booths that ensured privacy. He didn't want his conversation with Lydia to be overheard. He wasn't sure he wanted anyone he knew to see him with Lydia at all. There was something odd about her. He'd noticed it every time they met. But with his reputation and his ability to lead on the line, he had no choice but to stay in this agreement with her.

He smelled her musk-scented perfume before he saw her. She plopped down onto the booth seat opposite him and gave what he thought was supposed to be a flirtatious smile. She really looked like she had a bad case of gas, but he'd give her the benefit of the doubt.

"Hello, Lydia." He nodded his head in greeting.

"Isn't this a beautiful day?" Lydia sat her purse beside her and readjusted her body on the seat. "The drive here was beautiful. There's such lovely countryside between here and Hempstead. Oh, wait.

You have to drive mostly through the city, don't you?"

Al's hands tightened under the table. So that's the direction they were going, huh? He toyed with the idea of offering a brilliant retort but decided to be nice. He didn't have to stoop to her level.

"A little," he said. "But the budding trees and spring flowers were dazzling as I drove along the park."

"Oh, I love lilac season." Lydia sighed. "The air is so sweet and the colors touch my soul. There was a lilac bush outside my bedroom window when I was a child. I still get a little nostalgic when the first blooms come."

As the kids said, TMI. Way too much information. Yet despite his best efforts, his mind drew a mental picture of a younger Lydia Willowood mooning around a backyard bush. No wonder she was a little loopy.

"What a pleasant memory," he said before changing the subject entirely. "I hear the chicken pot pie is quite good."

"Oh, I adore chicken pot pie."

Al silenced a sigh as she launched into a description of the dinners her grandmother made

197

back on the farm. For Pete's sake this was a business meeting, not a…

Good heavens, could the woman think he'd asked her on a date? Sudden fear paralyzed him. She was exactly the kind that would become a stalker. He didn't want to end up on one of those reality crime shows with a re-creation of how she broke into his house and whacked him to death with a machete.

"…and that was nothing compared to her lemon pie. The meringue was three inches thick and so delicious."

Al realized he'd zoned out. Apparently she'd been talking the whole time about her grandmother's cooking. He looked back down at the menu and said, "Oh, they also have chicken salad croissants." Surely the woman's family didn't make those, too. "And a fruit plate that sounds interesting."

He could have jumped up and kissed the waitress who appeared to take their drink order. That break let him reorganize and start a much more appropriate conversation.

"So what's new with the Greene girl?" he asked.

Lydia gave a dismissive wave. "Let's not spoil a nice meal with business. I so rarely am able to leave my kids that this is a real treat. You'd be surprised how much they depend on me."

That much was true. Al had heard from various teachers that Lydia Willowood was best at sitting behind her desk and micro-managing student schedules. Hempstead turned out a steady stream of students who were able to earn a living as soon as they graduated. The girls became bank tellers and office workers; the boys were mechanics, gardeners and computer repairers. He figured a trained monkey with a rubber stamp could do her job for a few bananas a day.

But right now he needed her. So he listened in pained silence, attempting to get a few words in when he could. Their food arrived soon after the waitress took their order and Al attempted to eat in silence. That, it turned out, was impossible when dining with Lydia.

"My high school music teacher said I was the most talented vocalist he'd ever trained," she said with no sign of modesty. "He insisted I should attend a European music academy to truly develop my voice, but I already had that deep hunger to help children."

For a moment, Al was afraid she was going to burst into an opera aria right here among the chicken decorations and checkered tablecloths. To his relief she settled for humming something he thought was a show tune from when she was younger. He wasn't sure; it could have been a bumblebee's drone for all the music it had.

He expected her to lick the plate when she finished the last of the baked steak dinner that came with mashed potatoes and gravy, green beans, corn and a fat chunk of cornbread. The woman could certainly put away food. He'd ordered the same and only managed to eat half of his.

"Would you care for dessert?" The question came as the waitress picked up their dirty plates.

"Oh, yes."

Al noticed a certain glee in Lydia's voice.

"Would you have lemon meringue pie by any chance?"

"I'm afraid not, but we do have peanut butter, coconut cream, raspberry, apple, cherry, and peach cobbler. Or you might like to try our triple chocolate cake. All our desserts are baked right here."

Al declined while Lydia mulled her choices. He wasn't surprised when she couldn't decide which sounded best and instead ordered both chocolate cake and the cobbler.

"Oh, and please bring two forks." Lydia simpered in Al's direction. "We'll be sharing."

Al had no intention of sharing anything with Lydia Willowood, not even chocolate cake. He was here for one reason and one reason only: To keep Violet out of the spelling bee. Or, if that failed, to make sure she washed out on the very first round and in a big way.

He suffered through Lydia's account of her college roommate's attempts at cooking until both desserts were gone. After the table was cleared and they had refills of coffee, he put his hands on the tabletop and leaned forward.

"Lydia," he said in a clear and distinct voice, "what are we going to do about that girl?"

"Suggest something and I'll make it happen." She poured more cream and emptied three sugar packets into her cup. "I've tried and tried, but there's nothing I can use to stop her. Her grades are excellent, she's on top of her homework and she's even become a teacher's assistant because of her willingness to help and her good attitude. If she would do one tiny thing wrong, I could punish her by taking her out of the spelling bee. And trust me, I've been looking."

The moment Al heard the words "trust me" he was suspicious. Right now he suspected Lydia could be trying harder by getting out of her office and spending a little more time in observation.

"She's never gotten in an argument with another student or her roommate?"

Lydia shook her head. "She's in a single, and she seems to be friends with everyone. That's her personality."

"Problems with a teacher?"

"Afraid no." Lydia sighed. "She was terrible in cooking and office machines, but the teachers loved her because she tried so hard."

"Hasn't she broken any rules in all these weeks?" Al's voice rose in exasperation.

"Lower your voice!" Lydia hissed. "You're drawing attention."

Al leaned toward her and whispered loudly, "Are you telling me the girl is perfect?"

"Close to it. So let's come up with something besides my leveling a false charge against her."

Al sat back and so did Lydia. Seconds later she excused herself and headed for the ladies room.

Al closed his eyes and drew in a deep breath. He needed to calm himself or he'd end up strangling the woman right here in public. He visualized himself on a warm sunny beach on a tropical island. Palm trees waved their fronds overhead. Clear blue water lapped against the shore. He lay on a chaise with the only worry on his mind whether to motion for another tall, cool drink or take a nap in the sunshine. He was at the point of inner peace when Lydia's voice interrupted with "Hey, don't go to sleep on me!"

He opened his eyes. She had the look on her face again. Now he was sure it was her attempt at a flirty smile, which was far scarier than effective. He straightened up and cleared his throat.

"As I was saying, we need to find a way to divert the Greene girl from the competition. She doesn't have allergies that might cause her to miss, does she?"

"I'll check her medical records, but she's been healthy as a horse since she joined us. Any other ideas?"

"What about the ones who recommended her? Can you call on them for help?"

Lydia rolled her eyes. "Not at Hempstead. Our goal, remember, is to help every student achieve their maximum potential."

Al steepled his hands and thought for a moment.

"You are sure she possesses magic, correct?"

"I've never seen anything but that doesn't mean I'm wrong."

"Hmm. No accidental lifting of a pencil or bringing something to her instead of going after it?"

"Never," Lydia said. "And I've been watching."

"Then how can she possibly compete?"

****

Lydia had been asking herself that question. She had arrived at a theory that made sense. She took a brave breath and said, "I think she knows she can't."

"Then why enter?"

Ah, there it was. Why would a student from a specialized school for the non-magical want to enter the spelling bee? She'd mulled that over ever since getting the notification of Violet's acceptance.

"I believe it's a political statement," she said. "Now I know the girl doesn't seem like a radical, but you know how teenagers are. When I was her age, I was all for saving the earth. My parents got sick of me telling them to recycle and reuse. Of course, I grew out of that. Oh, I try to be conscious of the environment, but I still enjoy my coffee in foam cups."

"A statement." Al drew out the syllables as if contemplating what she meant. Lydia wanted to shake him. He'd been a principal for how long now and he still didn't seem to realize that the quiet kids are the ones to watch. She knew Violet had been unhappy about being transferred and displeased at seeing her life plans changed. If some sort of rebellion about coming to Hempstead simmered under the surface, the perfect place to let it out would be at the most prestigious all-district event of the year.

"As in no kid should be singled out and that crap." Lydia slapped a hand over her mouth. "Sorry. I meant to stay stuff."

"Of dissent," Al said as though he hadn't even heard her.

"I wouldn't put it past her to get up there and announce that not only does she not possess a single bit of natural magic, but that it's unfair to discriminate against someone like her."

"Can you say that again?" Al looked confused.

She decided on a simpler explanation.

"Violet didn't want to leave her school. She doesn't believe that magical ability is the primary factor on school selection. She wants to rally others behind her cause."

"Oh. Oh, my."

"Precisely. The girl will make a laughingstock out of the academy and its fine heritage."

"Or a laughingstock of us." Al shook his head. "If she is persuasive enough, parents will begin to ask questions. We'll be forced to keep the substandard kids and create a program for them. Our test scores will drop, and my career will be under fire."

"And they'll close the academy."

That was more than Lydia could bear. She had a cushy job as counselor at Hempstead. Any challenge she handed off to Elizabeth Kalazmenthian. That's why there was a psychologist on staff, to handle problems bigger than a night or two of homesickness. She looked up at Al with wide eyes.

"Violet's been doing some therapy with Miss Kalazmenthian," she said. "Let me go back and have a long talk with the woman. I'll find out what's going on in that child's head."

"There are confidentiality rules," Al reminded her. "She won't talk to you about their sessions."

"Think what you want. The two of us are like this." Lydia held up two fingers twisted together. "By the weekend Violet will be withdrawing her name."

She left the restaurant with a lighter spirit than she'd had for quite a while. Two weeks from tomorrow the contestants would begin the first round of the spelling bee. And she'd make sure Violet Greene was still at Hempstead and newly reminded of how terrible failure feels.

Chapter Thirteen

"I'd like to discuss a student."

Somehow I just knew Miss Willowood was talking about me. I'm sure she thought she was being quiet when she pulled Miss Tiddums aside near the study room, but I could hear her fine. So could Raz who was walking beside me. When I looked up at him, I could tell he thought she might be talking about him.

Or maybe both of us. Miss Willowood had scolded him at breakfast about fooling around to amuse his friends. He tried to explain that he accidentally stepped on the untied lace of his shoe and would have tripped if Ollie hadn't grabbed him. She had dismissed that explanation with a sniff and a stern warning not to do it again. I could not believe that as long as he'd been in this place, Miss Willowood hadn't noticed yet that Raz was clumsy personified. He'd been quieter than usual while he ate his eggs and oatmeal but the others had made up for it, so I didn't worry about it long.

I wasn't the only student Miss Tiddums was intensively counseling. I know Wendy had been seeing her to talk about how she was going to cope with being home all summer and other students disappeared from class sometimes. A horrible thought struck me. Maybe Wendy's folks had changed their minds and weren't going to let her come back to Colorado at all. I made up my mind to ask my parents if she could stay with us. Nobody should have to stay in this place all year around.

Thinking about Mom and Dad made me remember that parents' weekend was in four more days. And like it or not, I had to tell them about the spelling bee. I mean that I was in it. They already knew all about the event because the kids of their country club friends always did pretty well. They were the only ones with a big failure in that department.

I so did not know how to tell them. No way would they believe that I'd suddenly developed mad magic skills at my age, but I couldn't let them know what was going on. I made up my mind to talk to

Miss Tiddums about it at the next so-called counseling session we had.

I couldn't believe she told me to be sneaky about it. I was sitting on the couch eating a blueberry muffin to fortify myself for my latest attempt at levitation when I posed the question.

"You could tell them the truth, but I wouldn't recommend it," she said after a long pause. "Your parents are interesting and charming. They're also intelligent enough to know that you're not the kind of kid to hide something like that in order to frustrate them. Magic is commonplace in your household, I'm sure."

I nodded and swallowed my last bite of muffin.

"My dad's always making the refrigerator open and a beer come to him during the ball game," I said. "And Mom hasn't put away a dish with her own two hands in years. That's why they tried to keep me at Green Hills. Mom said I might just be developing slowly. I guess they finally had to face the truth."

I swallowed the lump in my throat. I kept seeing my dad's face and the tears in Mom's eyes when they signed the papers in Mr. Winters' office. All that work they'd done with me at home had just proved I was nothing like them. A horrifying thought struck me. When I asked for a little sister, Mom said they couldn't have any more kids after me. Maybe they couldn't have any at all and so they adopted me. That would explain why I was so deficient in what came easily to almost everyone else.

They must have been devastated to find out about me. No wonder they tried so hard with me and kept me at Green Hills as long as they could. Of all the children in the world, they picked one who could never fit in.

I had myself really close to believing that until I realized there were pictures in the family album of my mom pregnant, supposedly with me. And there was that tiny nursery bracelet with Baby Girl Greene on it and my mom's ID number. Plus my lack of hair until I was almost a year old had made me look like a mini version of my balding dad. Even I could see that from my baby snapshots.

"But then they'll know I've been lying to them."

"Violet, you haven't lied. You've not told them everything going on in your life, and that's okay. Every person has a right to keep secrets, even young people."

211

"Really?" I thought it was a law or something that your parents had to know every detail of your life. They asked about it enough.

"Really." Miss Tiddums gave an emphatic nod. "Would you like to do a little role playing to help you figure this out?"

I nodded. I was willing to try anything.

Miss Tiddums sat on the end of the couch, all prim and proper.

"I'm your mother," she said. "Tell me that you're going to be in the spelling bee."

Oh gosh, I didn't even know where to start. If I couldn't tell someone who already knew, then how was I going to tell someone who didn't? I blew out a long breath and made a stab at it.

"You know the district spelling bee?" I started.

"Yes, dear," Miss Tiddums nodded.

"Well, Hempstead is going to have someone in it for the very first time."

"Oh, really?" Miss Tiddums acted surprised. "Is it someone I know?"

"Yeah, me." I braced myself for a "darling, I'm so proud of you" and maybe a hug. Instead I got a totally different response.

"But Violet dear, you're the least magical person I know."

Wow. Miss Tiddums had looked so pleasant as she stabbed that knife in my back. I sat like a lump, fighting back tears and trying to figure out what to say next. I hoped she'd give me a clue, but it didn't happen. She sat like a little bird on a fence and stared at me.

"What am I supposed to say?" I finally asked.

"That, dear child, is something you're going to have to figure out for yourself." Miss Tiddums stood and made her brisk way to the kitchen. I heard the sound of cabinets and drawers opening and closing so I wasn't surprised when she came back with two plates of peanut butter pie and two glasses of milk. Seemed like her answer to everything was food. And I was fine with that.

Eating gave me a chance to think. What was I going to say? Miss Tiddums was right. I didn't have to tell anyone what was going on unless I wanted to. But I kinda thought I'd like my parents to know. So with the empty plates and glasses on the coffee table I said, "Be my mom again."

Miss Tiddums obliged. When she reached "you're the least magical person I know" this time, I was ready.

"Innate magic maybe," I said. "But while I've been at Hempstead, I've learned a different kind of magic. It's a kind you have to approve of. You've always told me that if I worked hard enough I could get anything I wanted. Well, I've been working hard at illusions and stage magic because I want everyone to know the kids at Hempstead aren't all that different."

Applause from the doorway greeted me. I turned my head to see Morry there and Raz beside him. Shock isn't the right word for what I felt. I'd worked so hard to keep this part of my life from Raz because I wasn't supposed to tell anyone, and now here he was.

"Mr. Morrison said you can do some really cool stuff." Raz pulled out a straight chair and sat backwards on it. "Can you show me?"

My heart pounded and my palms got sweaty. Doing my kind of magic for Morry and Miss Tiddums was one thing. Doing it in front of Raz was another. So I took my time getting the deck of cards and length of rope from my velvet bag hoping I wouldn't make a total doofus of myself.

The tricks went well. The rope danced across the tabletop, the cards reconnected and Raz seemed amazed when I made a ball disappear and then made it reappear from Morry's ear. His praise was nice, but those were simple tricks. When I got to the bigger ones, he actually cheered.

"That evaporating water had to be real," he said. "No way could it go away with a wave of your hand if it's not natural."

I gave what I hoped was a mysterious smile. I wasn't about to tell him the moves behind the stuff I'd learned since Morry talked me into this. I did a couple of fire tricks, but I didn't attempt levitation with him there. I wasn't ready yet.

We sat around after I was done. While Morry and Raz ate pie, Miss Tiddums explained what was going on.

"As you know, each student has his own bag of magic just as band students have their own instruments," she said. "However, we recently found out that at times the bags are switched before the competition so the entrants will be working with a slightly unfamiliar object."

"And I'm in serious trouble if that happens."

She nodded. "We're going to make sure that doesn't happen. You worry about your hand work and we'll worry about keeping your bag safe."

Okay, that felt like cheating. But wasn't I cheating anyway? I pushed that worrying doubt away and listened to Miss Tiddums some more.

"Miss Willowood has asked me to meet with her tomorrow to discuss whether it's in your best interest to be in the spelling bee," she said. "I intend to tell her that you're having trouble accepting your lack of skills and that by attempting and failing, you will finally be forced to embrace the truth. I expect her to drag out the old chestnut of how failure is bad for you and for the school. I have an answer for that, too. You practice as much as you can and don't worry about the rest of it. We're all behind you."

"You'll do great," Morry added.

"I think you're brave." Raz looked right into my eyes. "I don't know if I would be able to even try going up there."

"Oh, trust me, no one would ask you," Morry said in a joking way. "You'd trip over the microphone, fall off the stage and put an end to the whole thing before it began."

216

I laughed with the rest of them. Having Raz know made me feel a whole lot better. I asked Miss Tiddums if she could call my dad and break the news. Having her explain it that way would be easier than me fumbling around. She promised to think about it and let me know.

Morry walked Raz and me back to the hall. They waited until I was at the top of the steps leading to my wing to wave goodbye and go to the boys' side. When I went to bed that night, I felt the best I had for a long time. This crazy idea looked like it was going to work. Even Alfredo agreed when I told him what had just happened.

****

"Have you talked to that woman?" Al had decided to eliminate small talk in his conversations with Lydia after she'd sent him a scented note thanking him for treating her to lunch.

"I will this afternoon."

Lydia seemed sane, thank goodness. And calm. He was grateful not to have to deal with her in a lunatic state again.

"Dig for information," he advised. "I still believe there's some chicanery here."

217

"I said I'll take care of it." The snap was back in the guidance counselor's voice. "You make sure that panel has some tough questions for the girl, and I'll get to the bottom of things here. It would be greatly to our advantage if the panel disqualifies her before she has a chance to get to a microphone."

Al was aghast.

"Are you asking me to throw the spelling bee?"

"Of course not. I'm simply asking you to make sure that every student belongs there. I don't believe that's such a difficult request."

The woman could justify anything. Al wasn't sure he had the same ability. His years behind a desk had led to a personal philosophy that he'd attempted to engrain in the students he was responsible for. Among its principles was that lies only led to more lies and eventual dishonor. Unless Lydia could uncover some plot that made Violet and her cohorts into villains, he'd be the bad guy if he stacked the deck against her.

As well as unemployed if it all fell apart.

"My powers are limited." Al pushed back. "The judges are independently selected from outside the school district. My basic contact with them is to welcome them to the bee, make sure they're comfortable and get them safely away at the end of the event before irate parents can find them."

Lydia gave a harsh laugh. "You led me to believe you had nearly total control."

"I became involved to help your academy from scrutiny that might lead to its closing. Perhaps you might do better on your own."

"Now let's not let our emotions get in the way of things." Her voice was soothing this time. "While you think about ways to weaken her success on your end, I'll keep a closer eye on Violet. If she so much as makes her bed without lifting a finger, you'll be the first to know."

"Good. And good night."

Al hung up before she could say another word.

****

"I can't do this."

Raz had led me to a kinda hidden place in the academy's formal garden, and I was trying to do the impossible: Lift my body into the air the way Morry had shown me. Twice. He made it look easy. I secretly wondered if Morry actually did possess magic and was trying to hide it. That would make more sense than believing it was a matter of misdirection and physics.

"You can." Raz grabbed my hand and stared right into my eyes. I stared back into his gorgeous deep blue eyes and began to believe I could. If the people I trusted most—Morry, Miss Tiddums, Raz—believed in me, how could I let them down?

"The worst I can do is lose." I tried to sound like I didn't care.

"Which will make you like everyone but the kid who wins the whole thing. There are going to be, what, a dozen people in it? You'll just be one of the losers and nobody will remember what you did wrong. They'll be like all ooh and aah over whoever gets the trophy."

Raz made perfect sense. He also still had my hand in his, which was where I was going to leave it. He was so, so cute with that dark blond hair that kept falling over his eyes and that smile of his. I wondered what it would be like to kiss him. I wondered if he ever thought about kissing me.

The sound of voices coming close broke us apart. I grabbed my literature book like I was studying while Raz moved a few feet away and pretended to be lying on the grass sleeping. Neither of us looked up even though the voices got close. When they started getting farther away again, Raz jumped up, and I stood up to join him. I brushed the grass off the butt of my pants. He acted like us getting caught wasn't any big deal, but I knew it was. If Miss Willowood knew we'd been alone together, here no teacher could see us, I could have said goodbye to my spelling bee days before they even started.

I knew she was watching me. It seemed like every time I turned around her beady little eyes were on me. Even Muffy noticed and she never paid attention to anything.

"Hello, Violet dear." Sure enough, there Miss Willowood stood right by the student entry door. "I see you've enjoyed the sunshine."

"Yes, ma'am." I gave my very best smile.

"Well, free time is over. Dinner will be served very shortly."

"Yes, ma'am," I repeated, resisting the temptation to curtsy. I'm think Miss Willowood doesn't get sarcasm.

This was casual Friday, so I kept my jeans and tee shirt on for dinner instead of the usual blouse and pants. It was a privilege just for juniors and seniors. I thought I saw jealousy on the faces of the younger kids watching us walk in. I could only imagine how cool next year would be when I was finally a senior. Whoa. I was looking forward to coming back to this place. That was totally amazing. I said so to the Terribles at dinner. We all began talking about next year, and that's when I learned that the seniors had a prom.

"With dates and everything?"

"Only if they're from Hempstead too." Molly leaned forward. "No outsiders are allowed."

Outsiders? OMG, I was one of them now. I was an honest to goodness, real Hempsteader who knew all the secrets of this place. Not that there were many. I probably had the biggest secret of them all, and no one even suspected. Miss Tiddums decided I didn't need any added pressure, so no one would know I went to the spelling bee until it was over. Which was super fine with me. I was nervous enough already. I didn't need a big bunch of academy kids yelling my name as I tried not to fumble every illusion I knew.

"So is the prom here?" I made myself get back into the conversation.

Ollie laughed. "No parents would pay what those tickets cost if it was. There's a country club like ten miles away, and it's always there. They even get a professional to decorate."

Now I was impressed. I could almost see the line of limos in the driveway by the front door waiting for the seniors to come out in their formals and tuxes. I wondered if Old Wishicould went along to make sure they behaved. I bet she did just in case some rich, lonely widower hanging out at the country club may be desperate enough to ask her out.

"Forget next year." Wendy waved a hand. "I'm dying to know who's going to get outstanding junior this year."

She laid a hand on my arm.

"I forget you don't know. The teachers pick the outstanding junior on grades, behavior, personality, and potential. She…"

"Or he," Ollie broke in.

"Or he," Wendy repeated with a foul look at Ollie for interrupting, "gets a trophy and their choice of rooms for next year. I hope it's me because I want that big tower room."

"Yeah, like it's going to be you." Raz rolled his eyes. "They always pick the biggest suck-up. Like Adam Troy."

We all slid our eyes toward Adam as one. I always wondered why he acted like he was so special and now I knew. He was the ultimate teacher's pet. He even made eye contact with Miss Willowood and told her she looked nice. If that was what it took to win, I was sure glad I wasn't in the running. I liked being just me.

We talked so much that I was still finishing my chocolate mousse when the announcement to report for study time came across the loudspeaker. I gobbled down the last of it and grabbed my book bag. I didn't have much homework to do, but I didn't want to spend the time in my room alone. Being with my friends was so much better.

Raz sat right beside me. I was designing an English garden just for fun when he slid a note over to me. I kept my eyes on my drawing as I opened it. The soccer coach was in charge, but I didn't want her to see me during the one time he actually looked up from his magazine.

You can do this. Raz had drawn a smiley face below the words. I smiled at him, folded up the note and stuck it in my book bag. I loved his notes. They seemed like something I should keep so that when I was an old lady, I'd still remember this spring.

Chapter Fourteen

It was time to harness all the acting ability I
had. Mom and Dad were walking up the front
sidewalk to Hempstead's front entrance. I could
hardly wait to see them; I missed them so much. But
another part of me wanted to run far, far away. I so
did not want to spend two days with them pretending
that nothing special was going on when the spelling
bee was rushing at me like a freight train.

I'd practiced hard last night but flubbed up
even the walking rope thingie. I talked to Alfredo
about it and decided my excitement over parents'
weekend was the problem. I had ten whole days to
perfect every illusion after they went home. Still I
slept badly. My dreams were about me being a
fumble fingers and Mr. Winters screaming at the top
of his lungs that I was a fraud and a very bad person.

Naturally Mom noticed the circles under my
eyes.

226

"Bill, look at your daughter!" She grabbed me in a giant hug and squeezed until I thought my lungs would explode. "She looks simply dreadful."

Dad eased Mom's arms away. He put his arm around my shoulders and gave a little squeeze, whispering, "You know how your mother is" before he let me go.

Mom was already marching away. I ran after her because I was so afraid of where she was heading. I'd just caught up when she spotted Miss Willowood and took off like an Olympic sprinter. Defeat enveloped me. I hung back and waited for Dad. Maybe Mom would be discreet for once.

Yeah, like that was going to happen. She was wiggling her finger in Miss Willowood's face and asking why her little girl had circles under her eyes and lost her spark. Mr. Morrison stepped in and calmed things down before fists started flying. I'd have told him not to bother because I was sure Mom could take her except everyone else's folks were coming in too. I so did not want to end my first semester here apologizing for my mother's temper tantrum.

"Violet is one of my best students," I heard him say as Miss Willowood beat a retreat to the dining room. "You should be proud of her. She can tear down a Briggs and Stratton engine and put it back together faster than most of the boys."

"She has always been good with her hands," Mom agreed.

I'd never seen Mr. Morrison that charming before. Or rather, Morry. I could definitely see his stage personality at work.

"And such a hard worker." Mr. Morrison was guiding her toward a quiet section of the corridor. "She's been my student assistant for the last month and done an excellent job."

Mom nodded. "One thing about my Violet, she's not afraid of work."

Dad and I kept walking toward the dining room. I figured Mom knew her way around the place by now. Besides, Mr. Morrison wouldn't abandon her. He's not like that.

"Remind me to send that man a new set of tools as a thank you." I caught the humor in Dad's voice and realized he was enjoying this. "Now let's see if they have any lemon cake in there."

He waved to Wendy when we went into the dining room. She was sitting with Raz and his folks. A warm feeling rolled through me. Raz was so nice

228

to share his parents with poor Wendy. When he winked, I realized he'd caught me staring at him, and I felt my face start to heat up.

Lucky for me Dad didn't seem to notice. He was too involved with the extra-big slice of lemon cake he snagged from the dessert table. I excused myself to get glasses of punch for both of us. I was walking back with them when Mom came in with Mr. Morrison. They were talking away as if they'd known each other forever. I was impressed when he escorted her over to Dad, a glass of punch in his hand. He sat it on the table and then pulled out her chair so she could sit.

"He is such a nice man," Mom sighed as he walked away. "I'm so pleased you're in his class, honey."

Dad and I exchanged glances. Mr. Morrison had saved the day.

"I think it's wonderful that our little girl will be able to fix our lawnmower," Mom rattled on. "Wait till I tell the girls the next time we have lunch. They will be absolutely jealous."

Okay, I knew she was trying to build up my confidence like those parenting books say to. I didn't care. Having Mom say good things about me instead of worrying that I was going to ruin my academic career felt great. I know I had to be grinning ear to ear when she sent me over to nab a piece of red velvet cake for her. This was the best parents' weekend ever.

I had enough points that I could do whatever I wanted with Mom and Dad. Still, we stayed at Hempstead that night to watch a movie with the other families. Wendy sat with us and shared my popcorn. Raz and his folks sat right behind us, and the other Terribles were close, too. Close enough that I realized we all laughed at the very same parts.

For a while, I forgot all about the spelling bee, finals and Miss Willowood stalking me. A little bit of sadness sneaked in when I realized this was the very last parents' weekend of the year. The next time my parents came, it would be to take me home for the summer.

Away from my new and wonderful friends. Away from, gulp, Raz. What if he fell in love over the summer and never came back? Even worse, what if he fell in love over the summer and he did come back?

I wadded that particular worry into a ball and tossed it to the back of my mind. Right now life was fantabulous. I wasn't about to waste a minute of it.

After the movie a bunch of us went out onto the wide side verandah. Summer furniture had been set up there so we kinda made our own little huddle. The moms started talking about recipes and Pinterest and the dads talked about golf and the start of baseball season. We Terribles talked about stupid stuff, like music and whether Batman could beat Spiderman in a fight. One of the kitchen ladies rolled out a cart with lemonade, iced tea and cookies. The way we attacked them you'd never know we'd already had cake.

My mom and dad were among the last to leave. Of course, they weren't as tired as some parents. They had a short drive. Ollie's parents drove almost ten hours to spend the weekend with him, and they never ever missed. I walked down to my folks' car and hugged them both before they left. I almost, almost, told them about Morry and Miss Tiddums and the spelling bee, but I stopped myself. Miss Tiddums said she'd call them a day or two in advance. I figured I could trust her to make sure they got there to see me.

"I'm proud of you, kiddo." Dad's smile showed me he meant it. "I know leaving your old school was hard, but you're doing great here. You have nice friends, your grades are good and you've got your old sparkle back."

I didn't know I'd had any sparkle to lose but apparently I did. I'm never sure what Dad means when he says stuff like that but I know it's all good. So I hugged him again just because.

****

As soon as my head hit the pillow, I was asleep. I woke up just in time to get dressed and have breakfast before they came back to pick me up. I had full privileges, which meant I could go anywhere with them as long as I was back by eight at night. Mom had this look on her face when she got out of the car that meant she was up to something. I really hoped she didn't plan to drag me all through the mall to buy summer clothes. The sun was bright, the day was hot but not too hot, and I was tired of being inside.

"Oh, good, you wore shorts." She smiled and hugged me hello. It seemed like she'd hugged me more since I'd come to this place than she had in my whole life before. "Dad and I have a surprise for you."

Uh-oh. I'd been through Mom's surprises before like the clown she hired for my sixteenth party because, she said, it was my last chance to be silly. Oh, yeah, that was a hit with the guy I was crushing on. He never called to ask me out and avoided me as much as he could at school.

I got into the back seat. Something went squawk when I sat down; I realized it was one of Waldo's squeaky toys. He might be in doggie day care for the weekend but his presence lingered.

When Mom didn't immediately launch into an animated conversation over Waldo's latest escapades, I knew she had something big in mind. It meant it had to be big to be more important than the stupid dog. I watched the road as Dad turned onto a smaller two-lane highway. We drove like forever and then a big wooden sign came into view.

"Valley View, The Place for Fun."

Okay, that got me excited. Valley View is like the coolest place ever. It's like a campground and water park all in one. Dad pulled up in front of one of the little cabins and said, "Surprise! Our home away from home."

I walked in and realized that they were staying here for the weekend. It was rustic but it had air conditioning, the one thing my mother absolutely cannot live without. When the thermometer hits seventy, the air conditioner at home goes on and stays on until the first snowflakes fly.

Dad tossed me a shopping bag. I opened it up and found the cutest swimsuit ever. Not quite small enough to be a bikini but almost; it had smiley faces all over it. They'd gotten me a bright orange beach towel with smiley faces too. I hurried into the tiny bathroom and put the suit on.

****

We had a blast. I can't remember the last time I had that much fun just with my folks. Valley View has this super fabulous water slide, and we must have gone down it like a hundred times. When I started to get hungry, Dad suggested I go over to the shelter house and find a table while he and Mom went back to the cabin to get food.

I couldn't believe the way they tricked me. I heard my name called as soon as I walked into the cool shade of the open wooden building. I looked over to see Wendy waving at me from where a couple of tables were pushed together. Raz was there with his folks, too, and Muffy and her mom.

"Is this cool or what?" Muffy rushed over and yanked me to where the others were. "My mom was like oh, I have a surprise for you, but with her it's something like concert tickets or a pony. I could not believe we all get to hang out together away from school."

"Away from Old Wishicould." I giggled at the thought of Miss Willowood hovering over us in one of those old lady swimsuits with a skirt to her knees.

"Hey." Raz greeted me and patted the place beside him on the picnic bench. I said hi to his parents and sat down. His mom had a big smile, so I figured Raz spilled the beans about us and the dance. I mean there's nothing so special about me that other people's moms wanted me to hang around their kids.

He looked like his dad except his father's hair was getting gray and the man wore socks with his sandals and swim trunks. They both had the same great eyes, and even their smiles were alike. It was kinda weird knowing what Raz would look like when he was old.

Mom and Dad brought enough food for an army. There were sandwiches, potato salad, three kinds of chips, a vegetable plate and a big watermelon. Muffy's mom added a chocolate cake and fried chicken while Raz's mother furnished the drinks. I was so excited to see real sweet tea instead of the regular stuff you had to add sugar to yourself. And it was really good because Muffy's mother had grown up in Georgia.

"Honey, it's a state law that a girl can't get married until she knows how to make sweet tea," her mom said with just a little drawl. "You'll have to come visit so you can experience my sweet potato biscuits and peach cobbler."

That got the parents started talking about how we should get together some time over the summer. We kids didn't wait for them before loading up our plates. We only had a few hours before we had to leave, and there was so much to do at Valley View.

I lost big time at miniature golf, but I managed to do my fair share of ramming everyone with my bumper car. We spent most of our time in the lake though. We did more horsing around than swimming, but I was mucho tired by the time the parents decided we needed to get out and head for Hempstead.

"Would you like to come back out here tomorrow or would you rather see a movie?" Mom asked as we started the drive to the academy. She sounded nervous. "I know we kidnapped you today, so we want to make sure you get to do whatever you want tomorrow."

"Today was perfect." I meant it. It was so much fun to be a real person again. "Surprise me again."

"That's my girl." Dad's enthusiasm made me think he was cooking something up. "We'll be there right before lunch to pick you up."

Muffy and Raz were saying goodbye to their folks as I got out of the car. I gave Mom and Dad a quick hug each and ran over to walk into the hall with them. I noticed that Muffy's face and arms were red. She'd probably feel her sunburn in the morning. Raz was like me. He just looked a little tanner.

We chattered all the way to the staircase that led to the wings. I guess we were a little too loud because Miss Willowood like popped out of nowhere to give us a loud "Shhhhh." She followed it up with

"We're not savages here, you know. Well-bred people use well-bred voices."

She sounded so much like my grandmother that I had to bite my lip to keep from laughing. I half expected her to launch into a lecture about running with scissors next.

Raz waved goodnight and started toward the boys' wing. Muffy and I hurried to our rooms because Miss Willowood's eyes were boring holes in our backs. I was tired enough to collapse into bed right away, but I knew what I had to do.

I locked the door just in case Miss Willowood decided to make a surprise visit and pulled my velvet bag from the box under my bed. Concentrating hard, I did every illusion perfectly. Except raising myself up off the floor. Morry was so wrong. No way was I good enough to pull that off.

Maybe it was sunstroke or maybe getting away gave me a new perspective. But I was done beating myself up over it. Floating in the air was a great trick, but I was aware of my limitations. Besides who knew if I'd even get far enough to need that?

I went to bed feeling super good. So what if I lost in the first round or even the second? I wasn't there to win. I was going because Morry asked me to. Because he gave up what he loved doing in order to teach kids like me. All I had to do was my best and we'd all be happy. Even Alfredo agreed.

****

"Bravo!" Miss Tiddums jumped to her feet and applauded. "I believed that was natural and I know better."

I knew I had a stupid grin on my face as I took a bow. I'd done different illusions every night and each one had been perfect. There were only five days to go, yet I wasn't nervous at all. Morry had changed locations every night because he said it would help me when I went up on the stage. He was right. The first time we went to the chemistry lab after dinner. That felt weird. Tonight we were in the research section of the library, and I didn't even think about my surroundings.

I knew Morry was dying to ask me about my grand finale trick. I'd told him after parents' weekend that I wasn't sure fake levitation was my thing. He was cool about it. He told me the choice was mine and he wouldn't push me to do it if I didn't want to. Miss Tiddums didn't ask me either, so I figured Morry spilled the beans to her.

239

"Tell you what, let's take tomorrow off."
Morry glanced over at Miss Tiddums. "That okay
with you?"

Miss Tiddums nodded, and once again, I got
this feeling that there was something between the two
of them. Maybe they were just good friends. But
maybe there was more. Which would be super
fantastic with me.

Actually our sneaking around worried me a
little. Miss Willowood had actually caught me
between classes to, in her very own words, "spend a
moment with my favorite student."

Or as I interpreted it, make sure I wasn't
doing something she could call me out on.

Miss Tiddums' presence was my security
blanket as we walked through the main building and
on to the girls' wing. She patted my shoulder and said
goodnight at the end of my hall. I tiptoed down to my
room and let myself in as quietly as I could.

I was already in bed when I sat up straight at
the horrible realization that I'd left my little bag
behind. Everything I needed for the spelling bee was
in there. Even worse, I had no idea who might find it.
I started to cry when I realized that after all these
weeks and all this work, I'd put the entire thing into

240

jeopardy. Hugging Alfredo close, I tried to figure out what to do.

I couldn't leave my bag lying on a public desk.

I had no way to get in the library to get it.

I was screwed.

Sitting in my pajamas, staring out the window at the moonlit lawn, I finally decided there was only one thing to do. I pulled on my hoodie and shoes, tossed Alfredo onto the bed and broke the biggest rule in the student handbook: I left my room after lights out.

Too scared to take a flashlight, I flattened myself against the wall until I reached the stairs. The table lamp burning on the table at the bottom threw enough light to make me nervous. Staying in the shadows as much as I could, I managed to get to the side door before a horrible thought struck me.

What if an alarm went off when the door opened?

I hovered there, torn between rushing back to the safety of my room and the unknown, until I finally realized doing nothing wasn't going to solve anything. I took in a deep breath, turned the deadbolt on the door and turned the knob.

241

Nothing happened.

I was through in seconds and closed the door behind me without a sound. That path between the main hall and the cluster of teacher's residences was even scarier at night all alone. It was okay where the moonlight lit up the stones but spooky where the trees hid the moon. I was super happy to finally reach Miss Tiddums' cottage and ecstatic to see that her lights were still on.

Sneaking around to the back door where it was harder to see me, I tapped lightly on the glass. I was just about ready to knock harder when I saw Miss Tiddums' face looking out at me. I heard the snick of a lock, and then she was inviting me in.

"Violet, what's wrong?" She pulled out a chair at the table and asked me to sit down. I was too upset to take up her offer.

"I have to get into the library." I could feel the tears welling up. "I left all my magic stuff in there. We have to go get it!"

"Calm down, dear." Her voice was gentle. She motioned toward the chair again. "I'll call Morry. He can run down and get it while you and I enjoy a nice cup of tea and ginger cookies."

Wow. Could my big disaster end this easy? Apparently so because Miss Tiddums hung up and said, "Morry will be bringing it shortly."

****

So they had been up to something. Lydia knew the girl would slip up sometime. The tragedy was that she'd sweet-talked two excellent instructors into putting their careers on line. Looking right and left to make sure they weren't hanging around somewhere, she slid her key into the library door and turned it to the left. Once in she closed the door and locked it again.

Slipping a small flashlight from her pocket, she began to snoop. She swept it back and forth looking for something, anything, out of the ordinary. The circulation desk seemed as neat as always. She touched the tops of the computers. They were all cool. Doubt crept in as she walked between the rows of shelves. So far everything looked just fine.

She was almost to the research section at the back of the room when she heard the door open and close. Her heart raced. Who was here?

Lydia hurried to the shelves and desks that provided a measure of secrecy. Tripping over an unseen wrinkle in the carpet, she grabbed the corner of a table to steady herself and felt something more than the smooth wooden surface beneath her fingers. She pulled it off and stuck it in her pocket before hiding as best she could between a tall shelf and the wall. Tucking her head down against her shoulders turtle-style, she waited.

Footsteps came toward her, the sound muffled by the floor covering. She breathed as shallowly as possible as the shadowy figure came closer. She stopped breathing entirely for at least thirty seconds when she recognized the profile of Mr. Morrison. She began again when she realized he was too intent on looking for something on one of the tables to begin to notice whether he was alone.

Relief washed across her when he turned and left empty-handed. She felt the small lump in her pocket, fairly certain he was looking for what she'd accidentally found. At the sound of the engines instructor leaving, she slid from her hiding place and made her way back to the door herself via her handy-dandy flashlight. The lock sounded as she turned the key and headed outside toward her cottage. She shook her head as she passed Miss Tiddums' neat abode. How the woman woke on time in the morning when she stayed up half the night was a miracle.

Lydia was certainly glad her life was more orderly. She simply could not stand unorganized fools.

The treasure in her pocket seemed to get heavier as she walked up the steps to her back door. She made sure to lock the door and draw the curtains before she pulled it out. She knew exactly what it was the moment she laid eyes on it.

And a velvet magic bag most definitely did not belong on the grounds of Hempstead Academy.

She studied the thing with disdain. The academy was a place for non-magicals, its mission to help them become comfortable in a world that wasn't always inviting to people with their inabilities. For people like her. She'd created a good life here. Granted, she had a limited bit of magic, enough to relight a fireplace log or stop a pot from boiling over. But she didn't have to use it here. No one looked down on her because she wasn't able to pour milk without using her hands or create mini-hurricanes on a visit to the beach.

Her duty was clear. She needed to report both Elizabeth and Mr. Morrison to the board. She should call the Greene girl's parents immediately to discuss the situation. She should toss this bag right in the garbage where it belonged.

245

Instead she called Al Winters, not caring that it was nearly ten at night. He'd been determined that she find some way to disqualify Violet. She could hardly wait to tell him she was holding the perfect solution.

****

"Do you know what time it is?" Al would have hung up on the woman but he knew Lydia would simply call back.

"Three minutes until ten." Lydia's voice was waspish. "If I remember correctly, I told you that I'd call as soon as I knew anything."

"It better be good."

"It is."

"Just tell me." His finger hovered over the phone's end button.

"I discovered a velvet bag in a place it shouldn't be. A velvet bag that holds tools for magic."

Al jumped to his feet, fueled by an adrenaline rush. Hempstead existed to offer a safe, non-magical environment for its students. Magic and the paraphernalia associated with it were forbidden. Unless...

"You're sure it isn't part of some teacher's classroom props?"

"Oh, please." Al was certain Lydia was rolling her eyes. "Hempstead has a zero tolerance policy. And you should know there is no subject here that even remotely involves a study of magic. That's something we prefer their parents discuss with them at home."

Of course he knew that. He was also aware that well-meaning teachers would sometimes break the rules with good intentions.

"Where was the bag?" he asked.

"I told you, somewhere it shouldn't be. And I found it after two of our staff members allowed Violet into a locked room after hours. That's what you want, isn't it?"

Al began to pace. That tidbit of information put a new spin on things. The rules stayed in place even if the end of the semester was near. Students could be suspended up to the very last minute. He grinned. Suspension would keep a participant out of the spelling bee and save his hide.

"You know for a fact that it belongs to the Greene girl?" he asked.

247

"I don't have a video if that's what you mean." The snappish tone was back in Lydia's voice. "But I don't believe either of the principal parties will throw away their careers for a child who just transferred in. You take care of things on your end, and I'll get to the bottom of things here."

As a plan, that was weak. Still it was better than anything they'd come up with until now. And, he was afraid, their only chance to save both his chances of promotion and the school's reputation.

****

I knew the worst had happened when Morry walked into the cottage. Miss Tiddums had convinced me everything would be all right. His face told me she was wrong.

"It wasn't there." He looked at me. "You're sure you left it?"

I nodded hard. "Absolutely positive."

"You didn't put it somewhere different in your room?" Miss Tiddums asked.

"No." I'd hidden the bag in the sweater box under my bed every moment that I wasn't using it. I knew better than to leave it anywhere a snooping guidance counselor might look. "Did you check everywhere?"

248

"On each table and around everything on them. I'm sorry, Violet, but it's not there." He made a wry face. "If it held real magic, I might suspect it took off on its own. I'm afraid that's not a possibility."

I put my head down on Miss Tiddums' kitchen table because I didn't want either of them to see me cry. All that hard work for what? So I could get kicked out of school if anyone found out it was mine. Morry losing his job when he confessed that it was really his, and I knew he would. He was that kind of person. And poor Miss Tiddums would tell the administration she'd been part of it, too. My being stupid was going to ruin everyone's life.

Thinking about my parents and the Terribles made be bawl. My folks had been so happy last weekend, and now I was going to break their hearts. And as soon as Miss Willowood heard, she'd accuse my friends of being part of it and wham! They'd be out of Hempstead, too. And Wendy would never have a chance of being outstanding junior and get to pick her own room at this place.

"It's going to be all right." Miss Tiddums was patting my back and saying what grownups always say when kids go crazy on them. "I'll go over before the librarian arrives in the morning and find it. I'd say it slipped under a table or you accidentally dropped it leaving the room. Now lift your head and take a deep breath."

She sounded so much like my mom right then that I did what she said. Miss Tiddums wiped the tears from my cheeks with her fingers and smiled at me. I tried to smile back but I'm not sure I managed. Morry stood behind Miss Tiddums; he looked as lost and helpless as my dad does when I have a major breakdown at home. Then he did what Dad does.

He asked me if I was okay.

Well, no. I was sitting in the school shrink's house in my pj's, my eyes were puffy because I'd cried so hard, and my entire academic past and future were about to be rewritten. But I knew what to say.

"I'm fine." I sniffed hard because my nose was starting to run and forced myself to look as perky as I could. "Miss Tiddums is right. She'll find it in the morning."

"That's my girl." OMG, he sounded exactly like Dad. I wondered if there was a book for guys on how to deal with stuff like this.

They both walked me back to the hall. Morry was headed that way, natch, but Miss Tiddums went

along in case I went nutso once again, or so I figured.
Maybe she was going to sneak back into the library
and look right now. I was sure she wasn't going to
sleep any better than me until the stupid thing was
found.

I whispered good night to them as I reached
the back door.

"Violet, wait!" Miss Tiddums' voice stopped
before I touched the door.

My brain was on auto drive when I left
because I'd forgotten the automatic locks on the
doors. As in, after curfew no one came in without a
key card. An alarm blared if someone tried.

Mr. Morrison swiped his and the two of them
hurried in right after me. If the office staff checked
the records, and I'm sure they did, it would only
show Mr. Morrison came into the building shortly
before midnight. No one would know I hadn't been
snug in my bed the whole time.

Miss Tiddums went as far as the top of the
stairs with me. She didn't say why, but I knew. In
case Miss Willowood was doing a secret mission
crawl to see if she could catch one of us doing
something wrong, I had an alibi.

****

Even though I was positive I wouldn't sleep at all, I did. I woke up before the now-familiar announcement to get up and get ready for the day. The very first thing I thought about was whether Miss Tiddums had sneaked into the library again and found my flipping bag of tricks. As I took a fast shower and wavered between wearing the white shirt or the other white shirt, I went back and forth between total hope and crushing despair.

Hope was in control when I slipped into my chair for breakfast head count. Raz gave me a look, but the other Terribles didn't seem to notice. They were all yakking about stupid stuff like whether we'd really have to sit through every final if we got done early and how cool it was gonna be when we were seniors at last.

"We will rule this school," Muffy said with typical Muffy enthusiasm. "Hempstead will never forget us. Every future class will have to live up to our reputation."

Ollie rolled his eyes, and Molly laughed. There weren't enough kids here for a pecking order. There were like fifteen kids in each grade; although, our junior class was the biggest. Of course, that was only because I'd transferred in. Hempstead was so different from Green Hills where there were three hundred juniors who hardly knew each other.

Looking at the faces around me, I started to slide back into despair mode. If the bag had fallen into the wrong hands, I'd never see them again. The next step would be juvie jail where I'd have to wear an ugly orange jumpsuit and mop floors.

"Hey, you gonna eat?" Raz's voice brought me back from the inevitable future to the intolerable present. The others headed for the serving line. I shoved back my chair and went over to get a tray of food I had no appetite for. I wanted to tell Raz my crummy news, but this was so not the place and time.

I looked for Miss Tiddums, but she wasn't in the dining room. Hope surfaced. She was probably in the library looking in every nook and cranny. I crossed my fingers that one of those nooks or crannies would give up its treasure.

I went onto autopilot from class to class, too distracted to pay attention. My nerves were ready to snap by the time I walked into Mr. Morrison's class. He looked exactly as he always looked, which was no help. A clue, like a big smile and a V for victory, would have been fantastic. Instead he directed me toward a torn-up tiller and told me to diagnose the problem.

Getting my hands into its guts was what I needed. All my worries faded away as I unbolted this and took apart that. I jumped when the announcement came to change classes. Time had flown by, as they say. I had just enough time to use orange goop on my hands to get the grease off before I had to be in horticulture class. Time went fast there, too, as we transplanted the plants we'd grown from seed into pots.

I walked into the common room for free time and, big surprise, there was Miss Willowood waiting for me. Watching for me, I guess, because she never came right up to me. Her eyes bored holes in me everywhere I went. I tried to play a board game with Raz and a couple of the other Terribles but gave up. No way could I concentrate with that stare fixed on me.

The announcement to report for dinner let me escape. I expected her to fall in behind us, but she stayed in the hall. A little voice inside me whispered, *She's waiting for Miss Tiddums*.

I picked at my dinner and said "Uh huh" and "Yeah" when the conversation lulled. Mostly I watched for Morry and Miss Tiddums. They came in a few minutes apart and sat at different teacher's tables. Neither of them looked like they were being marched to the executioner.

By the time study time rolled around, I'd convinced myself that everything was peachy keen. One of them had found the bag. I'd get a little lecture about being more careful as if I hadn't already learned my lesson.

Curfew came. I went to my room. I got ready for bed and sat at my desk, trying to read but not making any sense of the words. Then came the rap at the door.

My pulse went whump-whump-whump as I took a deep breath and opened it to face my fate. I let out a huge sigh of relief when it was only Miss Tiddums. I was already reaching out to take the bag when she said, "I couldn't find it either."

I sank down, expecting to hit the edge of the bed but landing on the floor instead. You know that phrase "Woe is me?" I was butt deep in my personal world of woe now.

We talked for a while. She tried to make me cheer up, but I knew that was the shrink side of her. The part in there that reminded me of my mom seemed as worried as I was. I pretended to believe her when Miss Tiddums said things would be fine, that I should hunt all through my room for the missing bag. And I'm sure she was pretending to believe me when I said that I was sure I'd find it before morning.

"The worst that can happen," she said, "is that it's disappeared into thin air. Morry says he can make you a duplicate bag. Not only will you have it for the spelling bee, you'll have it in time to practice a time or two."

I smiled as she left even though I was all doom and gloom inside. New stuff wasn't like my stuff. I knew the feel of every item, the touch when the rope began to rise. I blinked really hard and decided I was not, absolutely was not, going to cry again. Instead I did the calming exercise Miss Tiddums taught me when I first started learning illusions. Then I closed my eyes and pretended I had the bag in my hand. I imagined myself pulling out one accessory after another, performing one illusion after another. Weird as it sounds, it was like I had my hands on each item.

I slept with both Alfredo and the other stuffed animals my mom had given me since I got here. I had

256

them tucked around me like good luck charms as I snuggled between the sheets and fell asleep.

****

"What to do, what to do?" Lydia paced from one end of her living room to the other, avoiding looking at the bag on the coffee table as she passed. She'd left two messages for Al, but he hadn't called back yet. She was tempted to put that bag back where she'd found it and let the chips fall where they might. After all, would anyone really believe it was her fault that girl was here? She'd relied on the test results she'd been given.

Al Winters should shoulder the blame. He was the one who'd sent her here after all.

Lydia was about to grab the bag and walk over to the hall when her phone rang. She glanced at the caller ID. The high and mighty Al had finally decided to get back to her.

She was slightly mollified when he began with an apology. She waited through his rambling explanation that when her first call came, he'd been trapped in a graduation committee meeting. She felt much better when he told her he'd cancelled his dinner plans in order to talk to her.

"I hope you have a plan," she cut in.

"Put the bag back."

"Excuse me?" Lydia couldn't believe she'd heard him right.

"Let her find it again. Once you know she's had time to hide it, announce a room check."

"Why would we do a room check?"

"I don't know." Al sounded impatient. "Say someone has a piece of jewelry missing. Or that a mouse has been discovered on that wing and you need to look for droppings in every room. Use some creativity, woman."

Lydia's fingers tightened on the receiver. Oh, how she wished she were there in person so she could give him a good smack on the head for being so rude.

"Once I find it again, then what?"

"Make a very public announcement that Violet Greene has brought contraband into your school. The district is very strict about unauthorized items found on school grounds. Any school grounds."

Lydia felt a little thrill. She could be the heroine here. The district committee would probably give her a certificate of commendation that she could hang behind her desk.

"When should I raid her room?" she asked.

"Check the rooms on that wing," Al corrected. "I believe tomorrow night. Producing it the night before the bee won't give her time to appeal the decision."

"The decision to ban her?"

"Exactly," Al said. "Exactly."

Chapter Fifteen

"Violet, can you stay for a moment after
class?" Mr. Morrison made the request like thirty
seconds before I was out the door. I figured he
wanted me to help search for the tools that always
seemed to get lost.

He motioned me into the classroom and, with
his back to the big window, passed me something
soft and familiar. My heart soared. He'd found my
magic bag!

"Where was it?" I peeked inside to make sure
everything was there. It was.

"Under a chair in the research section."

My excitement deflated like an old circus
balloon.

"But you and Miss Tiddums both looked all over in the library." I tucked the bag into my book tote.

"Which is why we're both suspicious." He cast a glance over his shoulder as if to make sure no one was spying on them. "We've agreed it's best if you don't store it with your possessions."

Oh. My stomach started to hurt. Why had I ever agreed to do this in the first place?

"We tossed a coin. I'll be keeping it until the bee."

"No." Miss Willowood had been breathing down his neck too. "All that can happen to me is that I get suspended. You could get fired."

"Violet, it's settled."

Like a miracle moment in some cheesy TV movie, inspiration struck when I saw Raz walking down the hall outside. He'd do it. Raz would hide the bag for me without a second's hesitation.

"Let me take care of it." I tightened my grip on the tote. "I promise neither of us will get in trouble. Cross my heart and all that."

Before he could protest, I was out the door and heading not toward my horticulture class but the other way. I walked as fast as I could to catch Raz before he got into his classroom. There wasn't time to explain. All I could do was grab his arm and whisper, "Meet me in our secret spot as soon as you can."

I headed the other way before he could blink. I was a couple minutes late to class, but the teacher was okay with it when I told her Mr. Morrison had held me over.

A bunch of stuff happened before the next morning, but I won't bore you with details. Let's just say Raz agreed to hide the bag where I didn't know and that I got very little sleep that night after Miss Willowood made us all leave our room so she and her team of custodians could examine every nook and cranny. I'm not even sure there was a rat running through our wing. I kinda think it was her way of torturing us one last time before the summer break.

Or she was trying to make sure I didn't get much sleep. She had to know by now that I entered the spelling bee. True to her word, Miss Tiddums had waited until today to call my parents, and I bet the first thing my dad did was call his good buddy Miss Willowood to ask about stuff.

Miss Willowood looked irate when she left my room and went on to the one next to me, the very last one to check. The custodians walked in with their brooms and sticks and poked everywhere in there, too. Surprise surprise, there was no rat.

"Go back to bed." She was grouchy. "And put your things up. An exterminator will be here tomorrow."

The next morning Wendy started complaining about being tired. Molly and Muffy did too, but not as much as Wendy. I pretended I was exhausted too. I felt good actually because I'd been spending an hour or so before bed practicing my illusions. I smiled at Raz who smiled back. Here we were with one more secret between us.

But last period I was nervous, nervous, nervous. Morry and Miss Tiddums were taking me to the civic auditorium for the district spelling bee. They wanted to treat me to dinner first, but I was too anxious to eat. So they promised me pizza when it was all over and my parents too.

Naturally, Miss Willowood had to say goodbye. I figured I'd hurry through dinner and rush out the door right after dismissal. But no. Old Wishicould stood right at the exit and waylaid me. She was all "We're so proud of you" and "The only failure is in not trying," but I knew it was all a bunch of bull poop. I could see in her beady little eyes that she wanted me to fail big time. Maybe fall off the stage and die of a concussion.

"Good luck." Raz was super casual as he said goodbye. The hug he gave me looked like it was super casual, but he managed to drop my magic bag in my purse that way. I gave him a goodbye smile and got into the car. I felt like dancing. We'd done it. We'd actually done it. Pulled off getting to the spelling bee, anyway. Now all I had to do was make the judges and everybody in the audience believe I had natural magic, manage to bluff my way into at least round two and not die of terminal fear before we even got there.

∗ ∗ ∗ ∗

"She's on her way."

Al responded with a hiss that made the hair on Lydia's arms stand up. It was positively reptilian. Surely the man wasn't able to transform into a snake. Or even worse, a crocodile with all those big, dangerous teeth.

"I did exactly what you said, but the bag wasn't in her room."

"You checked every inch?"

"Yes. At the cost of overtime for three janitors. There wasn't even a paper clip out of place. It's hard to believe that any teenager has a room that neat."

"So what do you suggest we do now?"

Ah, he was right where she wanted him. Desperate and in need of a plan.

"Don't worry," she lied. "I have it all figured out. Just be make sure you're at the door when I get there."

Al didn't push for details for which Lydia was grateful. She had a plan: Keeping Violet from taking the stage. What she lacked were the steps to make that happen.

****

Raz eased away from the door where he'd had his ear. He patted the device in his pocket. He'd bought it as a joke at a novelty gift store with no real idea of using it. The idea of a spy hearing aid had made him laugh. He'd never expected to use it for a good cause like this one.

The next hurdle was how to keep Miss Willowood from booking it to the spelling bee. Everyone he trusted was headed that way. Mr.

Morrison would know what to do. He was a genius at creative solutions.

He strolled back toward the front door. They were allowed to spend free time outside since the weather was gorgeous. He waved at the art teacher who was supposedly supervising but was actually working on a canvas set on a wooden easel. Heading toward a group playing soccer, he kept his walk slow and easy. When he reached a clump of bushes, he ducked in and used the cover to change his route. Minutes later he was among the staff cottages. He knew they were totally off limits for unauthorized students, Punishment would be swift and final. The school would call his parents and he'd be on probation until the semester was over. And more than likely, he'd wind up at some other occupational school next year. Some disgusting, dirty place where he'd train to be a garbage man, probably.

He pushed that from his mind and kept walking until he reached the faculty parking lot. Ducking down, he used the cover of her car to insert a screwdriver into the grille, pop the hood latch and ease the hood up. His knowledge of engines was coming in handy as he made a few minor adjustments that would keep the car from starting. Knowing Mr.

Morrison was consolation. The man could fix it the next day and it would be like it never happened.

Fortune smiled on him. As he made his wary way away from the car, he discovered a baseball lying in the grass. He grabbed it and headed back to the school lawns. He'd simply say he was retrieving the ball if he got caught.

****

Lydia couldn't believe it had taken so long to recognize what had been there right along. Students at Hampstead Academy were required to follow the rules. Students were not allowed to go off campus willy-nilly.

She'd kept the permission files. And she knew there was no parental permission slip on file permitting one Violet Greene to go more than twenty miles off campus, with or without a faculty member. And it was over 30 miles to the site of tonight's competition.

Humming, she walked toward the parking lot where her car waited.

She pushed the button to unlock the door, adjusted the seat and checked the mirrors. Turning the key in the ignition, she waited for the familiar hum of the engine starting.

All she heard was a click. She tried repeatedly but got nothing but a series of clicks for her trouble. Red anger began to rise, and she pounded on the steering wheel screaming, "No, no, no! This cannot be happening!"

Raz watched from his vantage point inside the clump of bushes. He couldn't see very well but he could hear fine. And not a sound came from the car Miss Willowood had stepped into. He thought he was used to not having a cell phone, but he wanted so bad to text Violet and tell her to beware of someone on the inside. Good thing he couldn't because it would only freak her out. Calling Morry was what he needed to do.

Instead he sat on the ground, surrounded by leafy branches, tossing the lucky ball from hand to hand. Feeling like a stupid kid, he made a wish on it that everything would go perfect for Violet tonight. It wasn't much but it would have to do.

****

"Miss Greene. How nice to see you again."

Mr. Winters said the right words, but his eyes were…something. Suspicious? Maybe. More like he was waiting for something. Which, I figured, was my quick demise. As a contestant, I mean. He never struck me as the murdering type. He's a basset hound, after all, not a pit bull.

I opened my magic bag so the check-in lady could look inside. I must have looked cool as a cucumber because she didn't ask me to take anything out. She put it in a plastic box, sealed it magically, and then my name appeared on it with nobody writing. The little thread of doubt that had been coiling around my insides tightened. Everybody in the world could do natural magic but me. Well, almost anyone as I remembered the Terribles. I focused on how excited they'd be to learn I'd been in the spelling bee. I knew they'd be mad that I didn't tell them, but they'd understand when they learned why it had to be secret.

My heart sank when I realized I was unlucky contestant number thirteen. That doubt began to grow and push away all the good feelings Miss Tiddums had instilled in me. My spirits rose when a guy came running up all apologetic and handed his bag to the registration lady. I recognized him as last year's winner, which gave him the opportunity to choose his spot. He asked to be first which meant I was now number fourteen.

269

I was nervous watch the others go in and face the judgments. I was ready to run by the time my number was called. Yet I took a deep breath and put one foot in front of the other

Walking into that room was like stepping in front of a firing squad. These people held my spelling bee life in their hands. One goof-up on my part and they could disqualify me from spell casting. I plastered on a smile and introduced myself like Morry told me I should.

By the third question my nerves had settled down. I was ready when the bald guy with the ugly tie threw out question number four.

"Miss Greene, please name two immutables."

I could hardly stand still. I knew this. I knew this!

"Time and space."

"Very good. Now please name the conditions of the second order of natural magic."

"Compounded, changeable and impure." I curled my hands at my sides to keep my composure. I knew I was right. I wanted to dance across the floor or shout a victory cheer.

"Very good." I knew I had to be smiling like a big goofus when the guy with the ugly tie stamped

"Approved" on my contestant card. Step one was over. Now all I had to do was go out on the stage in front of like millions of people, pull off perfect magic and manage not to throw up from being scared.

I did a quick head count as I took my seat again. Thirty of us. Being right in the middle of the pack was good. You weren't noticed much when you were dead center.

Mr. Winters hovered around like I was going to steal the cafeteria spoons. If he thought he was going to creep me out, he was wrong. I mean, what could he do to me now? He'd shoved me out the door of Green Hills without a second thought. It served him right to have to watch me shine.

See? I was doing that positive thinking thing Miss Tiddums taught me. I'd learned something at Hempstead.

I watched as one student after another took the stage. The kid from Ridge Valley fumbled his challenge to make a ball jump off on the floor, bounce and come back. But everyone clapped and cheered anyway.

Finally I heard "Number Fourteen, Violet Greene, Hempstead Academy." And I swear Mr. Winters went dead white as I walked out on the stage.

"I'm going to kill her." Al touched the cell phone in his pocket. He desperately wanted to call Lydia and ask her where the bleep she was. But he couldn't. The waves from electronic devices could interfere with natural magic, like microwaves blowing up pacemakers. He couldn't chance it.

And he couldn't leave. His duty was to ensure that no one got backstage or approached the contestants. His responsibility to Green Hills was to make sure that their representative, who had yet to compete, was calm and prepared to blow everyone else out of the water. His absence would be noticed and marked in his record. His permanent teaching record.

He glanced once more toward the door from the parking lot. Lydia should have been here long before this. She should have rushed in two minutes ago and put an end to this farce. Yet she was missing and Violet was unsealing the plastic box holding the bag he'd stupidly told that woman to give back.

He straightened his tie and shoved his hands in his jacket pockets. Well, the girl would wash out soon enough. If she even tried the first challenge.

Lydia had speculated that the girl was going to use the bee as a platform to denounce the separation of the magical and non-magical population. Al glanced toward the audience and began to prepare his response. He was the voice of reason, after all, and she was just a silly little girl mad at being sent away.

****

"Number fourteen, are you ready?"

I nodded.

"Then please demonstrate movement in an inanimate object."

"Would this rope be acceptable?" I held up the strand from my bag.

The judges conferred before announcing "Acceptable."

The dancing rope was a huge hit, bringing extra applause when I made it take a bow at the end. Even though I was super bubbly inside, I managed to stay composed until I heard "Passed to round two" from the judge's table. I wasn't sure where my parents were sitting, but I knew they were probably clapping harder than anyone else.

Mr. Winters didn't say anything when I passed him, not even the tight "Well done" he'd

273

given the last kid. Like I expected him to. Seeing Miss Tiddums give me an okay sign with her thumb and finger from the teacher's row was so much better.

I tried not to watch when round two started. I didn't want to know how much better all the others were. I closed my eyes and did the illusions in my mind. Morry's words came back to me. Somebody had to lose in every round and being eliminated early was no shame.

"Number fourteen, please take the stage."

I blew out a breath, told myself I could do this and went back out. I stood at the microphone and repeated the challenge when the judges gave it to me.

"Physical destruction and recreation," I said slowly before taking the deck of cards from my bag. "Will playing cards be acceptable?"

Again I waited as the judges conferred. And once more they said okay.

It was almost as if Morry was standing right there, perfecting my moves. I ripped the cards, scattered the cards, gathered them back up and then fanned them out perfectly whole again. And, yes, the judges did say, "Passed to round three."

274

Mr. Winters had a red face when I walked off stage, and he glared at me like, well, like I glare at Waldo when he tries to steal my food. I made a point of saying good luck to the Green Hills contestant. I didn't know him, but he seemed as nervous as me even if he had the real stuff.

Two kids failed to pass round two. That left eleven of us. No way would I make top ten, but I was good with just making it into round three.

The judges wanted me to make electricity. This one was tricky, no pun intended. Morry would not be happy with my spilling his secrets, but it involves a special light bulb and some aluminum foil. And it was good enough to fool the judges who passed me to round four. The kid from Center High couldn't create water so he was out. Which, ladies and gentlemen, put me in the top ten.

I'd never been in the top ten of anything before. I intended to savor this moment when I was an old lady, eons after everybody else had forgotten about this year's spelling bee.

I had about thirty seconds of that joy before Miss Willowood came bursting into the backstage area with daggers flashing from her eyes.

****

275

"Run, you little weasel," Lydia hissed as she stalked toward Al Winters who was heading for the stairs. She had to beg the keys to the academy's pickup truck from the head custodian just to get here. And when she'd walked in, what did she see?

Kids on stage. Kids competing.

Violet Greene competing.

The one thing Al was supposed to prevent.

Lydia's shoes slid slightly on the worn boards but she kept going. Her feet struck a hard tat-tat-tat as she pursued that worm Al. He clattered down the steps and fled down a hall. She was right behind him, oblivious to the spelling bee that had taken another victim.

"I couldn't help it." Al turned as she came upon him, arms out as if begging for mercy. "You were supposed to be here before it started.

"You were supposed to stall things."

"The panel went too fast with the preliminary questions."

"Excuses, excuses." Lydia crossed her arms and tapped her foot. "For a man who's been administrator of the year four times, you are most incompetent."

"Don't call me incompetent!" He smacked the wall beside him. "At least I'm not so pathetic that I have to hide away in a school with inferiors in order to keep a job."

"Take that back!" Lydia shoved Al and he stumbled.

"Will not." Al pushed back.

"I've never hidden from anything in my life."

"Including chocolate fudge and pie." D.

"Well, at least I have plenty of hair," Lydia retort

The argument might have disintegrated into a schoolyard brawl if they hadn't been yelling at each other. Two security guards, hired to make sure nobody got rowdy over the results, came running. One grabbed Al and one grabbed Lydia, who kept shouting as the guards pulled her off. She had Al's tie in her hand, so he came with her until the other guard managed to loosen her grip.

****

I tried to pretend I didn't hear the yelling. Some of the other contestants did too, but a couple of them ran to the steps to look. They came back and began to tell the story with excitement. The high I'd been riding on since making it through round three

277

began to fade. Soon everyone would know that the principal from my old school and the guidance counselor from my new one got into a fight. I hoped nobody figured out my connection to the two of them. My life was just starting to get good again. I did not need them to ruin it.

I missed seeing the cops arrive and take Mr. Winters and Miss Willowood away. I was on the stage with the latest from my bag of tricks, changing a cardboard square from yellow to blue. Even though I did it perfectly, I expected to get cut anyway. I mean, seriously, me going on up? Yeah, right.

To my amazement, by the time round seven rolled around, I was still in it with four others. The others were super good, though, so I figured it was adios time for me.

This was a contestants' choice round. I was getting low on choices. Actually I only had two. Either I could make fire on my palms or I could attempt to levitate. Safety versus risk. Making the sensible choice, as I had all my life, or embracing my reckless inner self.

I made my decision as I walked on stage.

"Your choice?" asked a judge.

"Levitation."

I sneaked a glance at Morry. He was giving me silent applause.

Okay, I know. This is where I'm supposed to give it my all and rise like a foot above the ground. And then I realize I do have natural magic and I'm not really a freak.

Sorry, didn't happen. My butt stayed firmly on the ground although my left foot went up a couple of inches. And yeah, it was nice to hear the cheers and applause as the moderator announced my elimination. Miss Tiddums was right. It didn't matter how far I went. Getting out there and giving my best was what mattered.

The best moment came right at the very end when the kid from Forest High faced off with the kid from Green Hills. They were both good. The Forest kid transformed a toy broom into a bouquet of peacock feathers. The one from Green Hills turned a marble in a plastic tumbler into a goldfish in a bowl. I have to admit that I was happy when that Forest guy got the big trophy and his picture taken for the newspaper.

There was this reception with cake and punch after it was all over. Miss Tiddums hugged me so tight I could hardly breathe, and I've never seen

Morry look so happy. My parents beamed from ear to ear even after I explained that my superior performance was illusions he'd taught me. I guess when it's your kid, it doesn't matter.

Morry brought a camera and got lots of pictures of me with my folks and Miss Tiddums and the other contestants. Then I heard a very familiar voice say, "Hey, can I get in one?"

I whirled and saw Raz and the other Terribles, rushing toward me, all talking at once and wanting to know why I didn't tell them.

"How did you find out? And how did you get here?"

"We're delivering plants." There stood the horticulture teacher with a huge smile. "Or that's what I wrote down when I checked out the van."

She nodded toward Raz. "This guy here figured you needed moral support, especially after Miss Willowood took off in the school pickup like a bat out of…heck. We figured she was up to something."

"Right now it would be putting up bail." I told them about Miss Willowood and Mr. Winters getting in a fight. Everybody from Hempstead started laughing, even Miss Tiddums who tries to be nice to everyone.

The Terribles helped themselves to cake and punch while the adults stood around and talked about how wonderful I was. I figured Morry could fill them in if he wanted. I had something else to do.

Like thank Raz.

I took his hand and pulled him over to a corner of the room where we could talk. I fished for the right words to tell him how cool he is.

"I knew you could do it." He spoke before I could.

"Oh, yeah?" There was some brilliant conversation.

"Really. A girl who knows her way around a two-cycle engine couldn't possibly be intimidated by magic tricks. Especially when she's smart and pretty too."

That's when I should have said something unforgettable. But I didn't because there was something better to do. Like tip my face toward Raz and let my lips meet his for the kind of kiss I'd been waiting for since the mid-March dance.

It was awesome, sweet and just perfect. Our
noses didn't hit or anything, and afterward all I could
do was look up into those eyes of his.

"So you my girlfriend now?"

I nodded.

"Good. Because I was afraid you'd forget
about me over the summer."

"No way." I caught my mom waving me over
from the corner of my eye. "Because we'll have cell
phones and Facebook and everything again."

"Even better, we'll have picnics." He looked
over to where our parents stood and smiled. "I've
heard a rumor that we're renting a cabin at Valley
View, right next to some people named Greene."

I smiled back. Life was good.

At least until somebody realized how many of
those stupid rules I'd managed to break.

Chapter Sixteen

The guy behind Miss Willowood's desk
looked friendly and out of place. Old Wishicould
might be out for what we'd been told were "personal
reasons," the academy's way of saying she'd put on

leave until fall. Which was good. Classes would be over by the time she finished her ten days in jail for public disturbance and the mandated anger management training.

Mom said she'd heard a rumor that Mr. Winters had decided on early retirement, effective immediately. Dad said he'd heard the school board had given him a bunch of money to leave. I knew I could find it out via my old friends once I got home. My folks were already planning a big welcome home party and they were inviting the Terribles too.

"I've heard a lot about you, Miss Greene." The name plate in front of him read Dennis Lackey. "I'll be filling in for Miss Willowood until school lets out and am joining the staff as career counselor next fall."

His smile made me sure Mr. Morrison and Miss Tiddums had already had a talk with him. I could hardly wait to get my schedule for next year now. Auto body repair, here I come.

If I wasn't getting kicked out.

"I listened in on a conference call with the district board this morning. The topic was this year's spelling bee."

Oh-oh. I braced myself for bad news.

283

"Apparently the other schools didn't read the rules as well as Miss Tiddums," he said. "Nowhere does it say only those with natural magic may participate. That loophole will be closed, of course, but you retain your runner-up honors."

I grabbed the sides of my chair to keep from hopping up and doing a happy dance. My picture would be in the paper. My folks could put my trophy on the living room mantel. Neither Miss Tiddums or Mr. Morrison would lose their jobs.

When Mr. Lackey stood, so did I. He shook my hand, congratulated me officially on my success and winked as he said, "You may want to review the school rules, however."

By now everybody at Hempstead knew what I'd done. Kids stopped to talk to me in the hall and even stuck-up Adam Troy high-fived me in the dining room. I even got an A-minus on my book report, the biggest surprise of all.

The last couple weeks of school went by in a blur. Between finals, working like crazy on the landscaping project and spending way too much time telling the Terribles everything I'd been hiding from them, it seemed like the last day of school came way too soon.

The big deal that day is the final assembly. Wendy was a nervous wreck. All she cared about was the announcement of who'd been picked as outstanding junior.

The moment arrived at last. Raz poked me as Miss Tiddums came to the microphone and whispered, "Look at Wendy."

She was perched on the very edge of her seat, fingers crossed and eyes closed. I could hear a faint mutter of "Please, please, please" and realized how much she wanted this. She stayed that way as Miss Tiddums gave the usual yay-rah stuff about how excellent the juniors were and what a great group of seniors we'd be next year.

Then came the announcement.

"For the first time in the history of Hempstead Academy, we have selected two outstanding juniors," she said. "The first student has a history of dedication to this school and a personality that makes newcomers feel instantly welcome."

It was Wendy. That sounded just like her. I looked over and saw her eyes were open now. Wide open. She knew it too.

She was out of her seat and running for the stage as soon as Miss Tiddums announced her name.

I was proud of Wendy. She managed not to cry until after she'd accepted the trophy and made the obligatory thank you speech.

I figured that tall kid from my English class was the other one. He toadied to all the teachers and always talked to Miss Willowood when he saw her. I figured he deserved it after working so hard at sucking up.

So I was beyond shocked when Miss Tiddums started talking about how the second student had proven her independence and love for the academy. Raz leaned over and said, "It's you."

Two seconds later, I heard "Our second outstanding student is Violet Greene."

I was no Wendy. I sat there, stunned, until Ollie said, "Go!" loud enough for everyone to hear and laugh about. When Miss Tiddums made a come-here gesture with her hand, I realized she really had said my name.

I blurted out something about appreciating everyone and everything at the academy. Wendy saved the day by grabbing the mike and saying, "Hands off the tower room, everyone. That's for Violet and me."

Another wave of laughter filled the room.
When everyone quieted again, Miss Tiddums
congratulated everyone who had been honored,
wished us all a great summer and said she'd see us in
the fall.

I walked slowly off the stage, clutching my
trophy with its laurel wreath on top. Mom would be
thrilled. She'd have two show-off pieces on the
mantel now.

"Mind if I join the celebrities?" Mindy linked
her arms with Wendy's and mine. "This has been the
best year ever." She giggled. "And next year, we're
the seniors. We will rule this school."

"Yeah," Raz said as the others caught up, "it's
going to be a very good year.

"But I bet this summer will be even better."

The End

About The Author

Cat Shaffer, the daughter of a poet and a teacher/librarian, grew up in northwest Ohio, finally saw the light and moved to Kentucky, the land of beautiful horses and far better weather. She lives with a dignified but ultra-sneaky cat and rambunctious dog, and could not continue to live if coffee disappeared from the planet. Check out her website at www.catshaffer.com.

Did you enjoy this book?

Share your opinion by telling your friends or writing a review!

Other books by Cat Shaffer:

Keeping Secrets, contemporary romance

Bittersweet, historical romantic suspense

Kentucky Blues, contemporary romantic suspense

No Safe Place, contemporary romantic suspense

Her Hired Man, humorous contemporary romance

Dixie White and the Seven Dates, humorous contemporary romance

Man of Her Dreams, light-hearted reincarnation romance

289